The Fury of El Tigre

El Tigre – the Tiger. That's what the Mexicans called him. His name was Jim Curtis, and he was a product of the Civil War, who went to Mexico to fight in the Revolution.

Now he just roams the West, riding from one town to the next – a drifter with no home. Then fate intervenes, in the form of a woman named Mary-Alice, and Curtis is soon up to his neck again in someone else's war. Only this time it has brought him face to face with an old friend.

The killers think they can beat him. But they've never come across the fury of El Tigre!

The Fury of El Tigre

B.S. Dunn

A Black Horse Western

ROBERT HALE

© B.S. Dunn 2019
First published in Great Britain 2019

ISBN 978-0-7198-2991-8

The Crowood Press
The Stable Block
Crowood Lane
Ramsbury
Marlborough
Wiltshire SN8 2HR

www.bhwesterns.com

Robert Hale is an imprint
of The Crowood Press

Typeset by
Derek Doyle & Associates, Shaw Heath
Printed and bound in Great Britain by
4Bind Ltd, Stevenage, SG1 2XT

For Sam and Jacob
and for George Snyder — still riding the range

PROLOGUE

Shiloh, afternoon
6 April 1862

Hell is a place on earth. Or so it seemed at that moment in time, what with the carnage of war surrounding the desperate Union troops as they fought for their lives in the place that would become known as the Hornet's Nest.

Up to this point, the Confederates had thrown brigade after brigade into the Hornet's Nest, and still the stubborn Yankees held on. Commanders such as A.P. Stewart, Shaver, Patton, Anderson and Wood, all sent their battle-hardened men forward, only to be thrown back by the resolute Federal resistance.

Then came the artillery.

Between fifty and sixty cannons commanded by Brigadier General Daniel Ruggles threw shot after shot into that stand of trees split by a sunken road. The once living, breathing vegetation was now a mass of shredded sticks only suitable for kindling. Amidst it all were the soldiers of generals W.H.L. Wallace,

Prentiss and Hurlbut.

On the right flank, Sherman and McClernand had already fallen back to re-form along the heights of a ravine.

Altogether, the Rebs had gathered some fourteen brigades. The Union troops were outnumbered, outgunned, and staring down the barrel of disaster.

'Captain Reynolds?' a soldier shouted. 'Captain Reynolds?'

Jack Reynolds fired another shot from his 1860 Army Colt, and the figure he was aiming for, dressed in Confederate grey and carrying a musket complete with bayonet, disappeared behind the cloud of blue-grey gunsmoke that spewed forward. When it cleared, he was gone.

'Captain Reynolds?' the voice shouted again.

'Over here!' Reynolds called back.

Hurrying across to the man he sought, the soldier found himself standing before a six-foot tall, power-fully built officer with dark hair and matching facial hair. The face was lined, and from beneath a battered campaign hat, steel-grey eyes stared out.

'What can I do for you, Sergeant?' Reynolds asked, as another Reb ball fizzed past his head.

'General Hurlbut has been forced to withdraw, sir,' the sergeant shouted above the sound of musket fire. 'General Prentiss wants this side of the flank refused, so as to meet the Rebs as they come on, sir. The general told the colonel. The colonel told me, and I'm telling you. The 14th Iowa will be on your right when you swing your line. Others will link to them.'

Reynolds looked to his left and saw that the flank was indeed hanging in the wind and the Rebs were gathering in force to try and roll them up from that side. His men, part of the 23rd Missouri, were now the left of the line.

More cannon shots landed amongst the Union lines, leaving big holes in it where men had fallen or completely disappeared.

'Shit,' Reynolds cursed. 'Take word back to the colonel that we'll refuse his line and we shall await further orders.'

'Yes, sir!'

Reynolds looked around his depleted line. Troubled eyes searched for his second-in-command, Lieutenant Lucius Frame. He grabbed a corporal from the line in front of him and barked loud enough for the man to hear.

'Find Lieutenant Frame and have him report to me. Double-time it.'

'Yes, sir.'

Somewhere further along the line, case-shot exploded and stripped a handful of men from an already thin line. To the Union front, a long row of Confederate troops stopped and shouldered arms. They sighted along their musket barrels, and upon command, fired as one, the sound rippling along a line soon to be consumed in powder smoke.

The cries of Union troops sounded through the din as lead balls found their target. One man had part of his face shot away, another took three balls in his guts. Even more took wounds that were ghastly to see. Ones

9

that would eventually cost arms or legs.

'Close the gap in the line!' Reynolds shouted at his men. 'Fill the damned holes! Keep up the fire!'

Suddenly, Lieutenant Frame appeared beside him. 'You wanted me, sir?'

'Yes. It would seem that General Hurlbut has pulled back and left our flank exposed. I've orders to refuse the line on the left before the Rebs roll us up. See to it. And make sure every man has some ammunition. The Iowa boys will be on our right.'

'Yes, sir.'

Frame hurried away and began to organize the line. It wasn't long before he had them turned at ninety degrees to the firing line and moving left to allow the 14th Iowa, 3rd Iowa, 18th Wisconsin, 21st Missouri and others to link in with them. They would be ready to meet the new onslaught when it came.

'Runner!' Reynolds cried out. 'Smith, on me!'

A young private with a grime-covered face came across to Reynolds, looking up at him with red and tear-filled eyes from the harshness of the powder smoke the firing line produced.

'Yes, sir?'

Reynolds opened his mouth to speak when a sharp crack sounded, and a Reb musket ball smashed into the private's head, making it snap to the side. The man fell into a heap at the captain's feet.

'Damn it,' Reynolds cursed. He stepped forward to the firing line and pulled a private out of it. 'I need you to find the colonel and tell him we've refused the line and are expecting to be able to hold the Rebs.'

'Yes, sir.'

Immediately to the front of the 23rd Missouri, the Confederate forces were starting to fall back. Not surprising, considering the amount of fire the Union troops were pouring into them. The lead being flung at the Rebs seemed to be cutting them down in rows.

Yet although they had withdrawn, the Union troops were still in dire trouble. Their right and left flank had withdrawn, leaving the centre to fend for themselves in a patch of wooded hell where the bodies were piling up fast.

Then as the Confederate forces gathered themselves for another assault, the cannons commenced firing again and steel rain once more opened large gaps along the front of the defensive line. Huge eruptions of earth shot skyward, and every now and then contained the remnants of a trooper.

When the cannon fire ceased five minutes later, Reynolds could see the enemy troops forming to their front.

'Get ready, men!' he heard Sergeant Jim Curtis shout. 'Remember, hold the line. I'll shoot any man who takes a backward step. You're the 23rd Missouri, and I'll not have any of you tarnishing that wonderful name.'

Jim Curtis was, of all things, from Texas. The men looked up to him, and Reynolds was pleased to have such a backbone for them to rely on.

There was movement at Reynolds' side and he turned to face the private he'd sent with the message for the general.

'Report, private,' Reynolds urged the wide-eyed man.

'The – ahh – the general sends his – ahh. . . .'

'Yes, yes,' Reynolds cut him short, 'get on with it.'

'The Rebs are getting in behind our lines, sir, and the general said to be ready to withdraw at a moment's notice.'

Reynolds was nodding when something occurred to him. 'Private, why are you telling me this and not the colonel?'

He'd not thought about it earlier when the sergeant had first approached him, and for that to happen meant. . . .

'The colonel is dead, sir,' the private said, confirming his suspicions.

Reynolds nodded, a grim expression on his face. What he'd give to be back home about now. 'All right. Find Lieutenant Frame and tell him of our new orders. Then report back to me.'

'Yes, sir.'

'One more thing,' Reynolds said, stopping him. 'Your name. What is it?'

'Hunt, sir.'

'All right, Hunt. Carry on.'

'Here they come!' Reynolds heard Curtis' shouted warning.

On cue, the trees filled with a rousing Rebel yell which was immediately followed by the staccato sound of the Union line opening fire. The men in Reynolds' company stood shoulder to shoulder, steadily loading and firing.

After the battle was finished, the Confederate survivors who fought in the place that would be known as The Hornet's Nest would recall of those opposite, 'The air was filled with so much lead that I saw a bird walking across it. There was no need for him to fly.'

Something tugged at Reynolds' left sleeve and when he looked down he saw a tear in his jacket. Although it wasn't the only one. He counted four others.

Reynolds noticed a concentrated Confederate push to the left, towards a gap that had opened tantalizingly wide. If they got through that breach then the line would disintegrate and the Rebs would roll up the line.

'Every third man drop out and move to your left!' Reynolds shouted at his men.

The cry was taken up by the NCOs along the line and almost immediately men were falling out of the line and moving to fuse the gap on the left.

Reynolds spotted Curtis moving with them. 'Sergeant Curtis!'

Curtis halted. 'Sir?'

There was a fresh cut on the sergeant's right cheek and a thin trickle of blood had streaked his grime-covered face.

'You hold that line,' Reynolds ordered. 'I don't care how. But you hold it.'

'We'll hold it, sir,' the Texan growled.

'Take care, Jim,' Reynolds said.

'That'll be the day, Captain,' the sergeant said with a smile, then noticed the captain looking toward the

Confederate line.

'See to the men.'

'Yes, sir.'

The crackle of musketry ebbed and flowed along the line and still the Rebs came on. Reynolds saw an officer out front waving a sabre in the air, encouraging his men onwards.

'Can't have that,' Reynolds growled.

'Corporal Murphy!' the captain called out.

'Sir!'

The voice came from in front of Reynolds where a tall man stood almost within reach.

'That damned Johnny Reb out there waving that toothpick around like a madman. You see him?'

'Yes, sir.'

'Kill him!'

'Yes, sir.'

It may have seemed cold-blooded, but that was the man driving the attack. While he was leading, his men would follow. If he was killed, maybe they would lose their way and the confusion would force them to fall back.

The musket in Murphy's hands roared. The distance was no more than thirty yards and the lead ball slammed the officer backwards.

Reynolds was right. Maybe the officer was well liked, or perhaps it was the shock of seeing their commanding officer fall. Whatever it was, the brutal death of the sabre-wielding man stalled their advance.

'Keep firing,' Reynolds shouted. 'Pour it into them, boys!'

Gradually, blue-grey gunsmoke increased throughout the wooded area until it formed a great pall which hung in the air, thick and heavy, filtering between the skeletal remains of the splintered trees like a ghostly mist.

The cries of the wounded and dying blended together in a bizarre symphony punctuated by musket fire. Reynolds managed to block it out. It was something one never got used to, but he was able to ignore it while focusing on his men and the desperate situation in which they found themselves.

Then another officer came forwards. Not as flamboyant in his actions as the one who'd just died, but coming to the front of the advance, he signalled the troops forwards, and started walking towards the Union line, six-gun in hand.

Reynolds felt a moment of admiration for the man heading towards almost certain death. But that's all it was, a moment. A fleeting instant, and then it was gone.

'Murphy!' he shouted above the next rattle of musket fire. 'Murphy?'

He was about to call the man's name again when he noticed him lying on the ground, arms outflung, a dark stain on his left breast.

'Damn it.'

He looked back up just in time to see the Confederate advance halt fifteen yards in front of the Union troops. Commands were issued and weapons were raised into the firing position.

Reynolds braced himself for the onslaught of round

shot and minié balls that would rip through his line, destroying material and flesh, even bone, with its violent passage.

He heard the call.

'Fire!'

Great clouds blossomed from the Confederate line as hammers fell on firing caps, igniting the powder, which in turn hurled the contained lead along the smooth bore of the weapon's barrel until it punched clear, searching for a target.

Reynolds flinched as a minié ball cut the air close to his cheek. Another tugged at a loose fold in his jacket, a third clipping the epaulet on his right shoulder.

Around him, the snap of flying lead filled the air. Men fell with balls buried in their bodies. One spun about with the lower part of his face shot away. Another soldier was on his knees, bent forward, clutching at a ghastly stomach wound from which his intestines were trying to escape.

Beside the mortally injured man, a fellow soldier bent down, said something in his ear, and then straightened once more. Reynolds watched as the second man drew a sidearm he'd appropriated from a Confederate officer earlier, and shot the first man in the head.

The men's names were Finch. They were brothers.

'Charge!'

The shouted order brought Reynolds' gaze up in time to see the Confederate troops begin their head-long rush at the Union line. Muskets were levelled and wicked-looking bayonets were now pointed forwards.

'Hold the line!' Reynolds shouted to his men.

With shrill rebel yells piercing the cacophony of other sounds, the Reb troops closed the distance between the two sides until, with an audible whoof, they came together and continued killing each other with a bloody and grim determination.

A burning pain cut deep into Reynolds' left side as a Reb bayonet pierced the skin and glanced off one of his ribs. He cursed through gritted teeth and brought up his Army issue Colt, firing point-blank into the snarling face of the Confederate soldier who'd tried to end his life.

The .44 calibre slug smashed through the man's teeth and blew out the back of his head. He crumpled to the ground and was immediately replaced by another soldier. Reynolds shot him, too.

One thing Reynolds had learned in his time fighting was that death didn't discriminate. It didn't matter if you were officer or trooper, general or private. If your time had come, then there was no avoiding it. To prove it, all along the line were blue and grey-clad bodies entwined as though in some macabre embrace.

Above the noise of battle, Reynolds could hear Curtis' voice barking orders as he organized those in his charge. He cast a quick glance towards him and saw the sergeant thrust his rifle butt forwards into the face of a Confederate soldier. The man dropped as though pole-axed at the Texan's feet.

Then from out of the mêlée to Reynolds' right came the officer who'd taken over the lead in the

17

Confederate attack. He was wild-eyed, and his grime-covered face showed a large scar that disfigured his right cheek. In his hand was a cocked sidearm, while his grey uniform had telltale bloodstains on it.

To his horror, Reynolds saw him approach Lieutenant Frame who was grappling with a Reb soldier, completely unaware of the danger approaching him. The Confederate officer raised the gun, and only inches from the young lieutenant's head, squeezed the trigger. Frame's head snapped to one side and he slumped lifelessly to the blood-soaked earth.

'Son of a bitch!' Reynolds snarled, raising his own six-gun.

The Reb officer must have sensed what was happening and turned to face him. He stared at Reynolds and then smiled a twisted grimace, made more so by the livid scar.

The hammer fell on Reynolds' Colt and the weapon misfired. A dry click was all that sounded from the six-gun. The Union officer cursed and thumbed the hammer back again. He squeezed the trigger again and the same thing happened.

Frustration took over. 'Christ.'

Unable to do anything, Reynolds watched the smiling figure turn away and walk into the mêlée, thick powder smoke enveloping him like a shroud.

'Captain! Look out!' Curtis shouted.

Reynolds whirled in time to confront a Confederate soldier about to skewer him with a wicked-looking bayonet.

The Union officer reacted instinctively and brought up the useless Colt he was holding and batted the pointed blade away at the last possible moment. The Rebel's momentum carried him forwards, close enough for Reynolds to reverse the swing of his gun and club it against the attacker's head. A sickening crunch was audible and the soldier dropped to the ground, convulsed, and died.

'They're falling back! Hurrah!'

The cry travelled along the line and Reynolds looked up to see the remains of the Confederate brigade fading away into the heavy mist created by the constant firing. Most were helping wounded comrades, trying to get back to their own lines.

There was movement beside Reynolds and a voice said, 'Captain?'

He turned and saw a sergeant. A different one this time. 'What is it?'

'The general says to organize your men, sir. We're pulling back. The 3rd Iowa will lead the way. Follow them through the gap in the lines before the Rebs close it.'

Reynolds nodded. 'Thank you, Sergeant.'

After the sergeant disappeared, Reynolds opened his mouth to call out to Frame. He checked himself and sought out Curtis. When he found him, the sergeant was crouched beside a man, checking the severity of his wounds.

'Sergeant.'

Curtis stood up and eyed his commanding officer. 'Sir?'

19

'We're pulling out. Keep an eye on the 3rd Iowa boys, we're to follow them.'

'Yes, sir,' Curtis acknowledged. 'And Lieutenant Frame, sir?'

'There's nothing we can do for him, Jim. See to the men and let's get the hell out of this deathtrap.'

'They're coming in on the left, Captain,' Curtis shouted from behind Reynolds.

The captain cast a glance over his shoulder as another volley rippled along the line in front of him. He could see the Rebs closing in, trying to snap the trap shut to cut off all route of escape for the vastly outnumbered Union troops.

'Got to hold it open for the rest of them, Jim. If we can't, the brigades that are left will be in trouble.'

The Confederate forces opened fire and once more the trees sang with lead. One of Reynolds' men crashed into him, half of his face shot away. In the distance, amid the fog of powder smoke, he could see a Rebel flag waving proudly.

Reynolds had split what remained of the brigade into two almost equal forces when the Confederates had tried to stop the Union troops from escaping. So far, some of the following brigades had made it through, but he knew it couldn't last. They were outnumbered and almost out of ammunition.

'Captain!'

Reynolds turned as Curtis ran up to him.

'We have to go, sir. The men are mostly out of ammunition.'

20

Reynolds nodded. 'Move the men out, Jim. We've done all we can.'

'Ahh, shit! We might be too late.'

A Confederate regiment had moved around their flank and was attempting to plug the hole that the Missouri boys were trying to hold open.

'Damn it. Get them moving. Now!' Reynolds turned to his men. 'Twenty-third Missouri! Withdraw!'

Immediately, the call went along the defensive line and the blue-clad troopers started to fall back, firing as they went. But they could only go so far.

'Sergeant Curtis!'

'Sir?'

'If we are to get out of here we have to break through that line of Rebs.'

'I'll take care of it, sir!'

He heard Curtis shout orders to the men in his charge and saw them turn from their front. With bayonets lowered, the Missouri men of the 23rd gave a roar and charged at the Confederate line like a human battering ram.

Before they hit the Rebel line it erupted with gunfire, and Reynolds winced when he saw more men fall. The Union troops faltered under the leaden onslaught, and looked as though they were about to buckle and run. Then he saw Curtis in the centre of the line, urging them to move forwards.

For a moment in time, the two lines stood there facing each other, maybe twenty feet between them. The Missourians cut loose with a weak volley that knocked a handful of Rebs over.

The Confederates countered with another of their own, and large holes opened in the line.

'Damn it!' Reynolds cursed. He leaned down and scooped up an abandoned musket and then cried out, 'Follow me, boys. Up and at the bastards!'

Reynolds led the charge forward to reinforce the disintegrating line. The Missourians with him shouted wildly as they ran. They reached their fellow troops and split through the line. As he passed Curtis, Reynolds shouted, 'Follow us, Jim!'

They punched into the Confederate line before another volley could be fired. To his left, Reynolds saw one of his men drive a bayonet into the eye of a Rebel who had already driven his own into the man's guts.

A corporal had his thumbs stuck deep into the eyes of a screaming enemy, his own wild with fear as he did anything he needed to do, in order to survive.

A large Confederate sergeant appeared in front of Reynolds. He had blood on the front of his tunic and a bloody tear on the right sleeve. His face was a mass of stubble with a line of blood flowing from his brow.

Using the musket as a club, Reynolds swung it at the snarling face in front of him. It smashed into the Reb's jaw, shattering it. At the same time the musket snapped above the stock. The sergeant went down as though poleaxed and never moved.

'Look out, Captain!' Curtis shouted.

Reynolds whirled just in time to see a Confederate lieutenant swinging a sword at his head. The captain ducked, pulling beneath the scything blow, which would have cleaved the top off his head had it struck home.

Still with the barrel part of the musket in his hands, Reynolds swung what was left at the lieutenant's knees. The impact was solid and a resounding crack could be heard as the leg broke. A scream of pain was cut short when the bayonet from Curtis' musket drove deep into the man's chest.

Reynolds nodded at his sergeant. 'Thanks, Jim. Keep them moving.'

Scooping up the sword of the fallen Confederate, Reynolds discarded the broken musket barrel. He looked all around and saw that his men were still heavily engaged. Behind the Missourians, he could see the gap had closed. Later he would hear that over two thousand men were missing, most of them captured by the Confederate forces.

Eventually, what remained of the 23rd Missouri broke free of the close quarters' fighting and fell back with Rebel troops close behind them. They crossed deep ravines and timbered landscape until they reached their lines. The Confederates had pushed them back some two miles. Behind them, Reynolds could hear the ironclads Tyler and Lexington firing on the Rebel lines as they advanced, until they were forced to turn back.

CHAPTER 1

Curtis was twenty miles shy of Abilene, and the war seemed a lifetime ago when he came to a small town in the middle of nowhere in the year 1868. By the looks of it, it was just a few buildings slapped together in a haphazard manner. Small lines of smoke drifted above some of the hastily constructed shacks, mixing with the oranges and reds of the looming sunset.

Curtis's horse was tired, not unlike the rider.

'I guess this will do, horse,' he murmured. 'We'll push on tomorrow.'

He nudged it with his knees and it walked on along the rutted track which led into the town. On the out-skirts, he found a sign which read 'Opal'. Later, when he left, he would wonder who could have given such a den of iniquity a name that represented beauty.

Curtis found the livery at the other end of town. It was a canvas tent with a corral out the back. It was run by Milt, a short man with a mouthful of blackened teeth. The liveryman studied Curtis, who was unsad-dling his horse. 'Nice bronc you got there, stranger.'

'I'd like to keep him,' Curtis said in a deadpan

voice. He turned to face Milt.

Curtis stood around six one. His solid frame was packed with rock-hard muscle and his square jaw was covered with a short-cropped beard. The brown pants and red shirt he was wearing were dusty from the trail, and his buckskin jacket was well worn.

Milt eyed him warily. 'Sure. He'll be safe here.'

'Good,' Curtis said, hoisting his saddle on to the top rail of the corral. 'If it rains tonight, put this inside your tent.'

Milt nodded.

'Is there somewhere a man can rest his head in town without getting robbed?'

'Anywhere outside of town,' Milt suggested.

Curtis looked to see if the man was joking but there appeared to be no change in his facial expression. He took his Yellow Boy Winchester from the saddle scabbard, grabbed up his saddlebags, and started to walk back along the street.

'Hey, stranger. That's three dollars for the night!'

Curtis paused and turned back to face the liveryman. 'If the horse is still there in the morning, you'll get your money. If not, you'll get something else.'

Milt swallowed hard. 'Sure, that'll work.'

'Hey, honey! Wanna give Delilah a good time?'

Curtis sighed. 'Show me your teeth.'

'What?'

'Show me your teeth.'

Delilah opened her mouth. All there, which was unusual.

Curtis looked down at her ample breasts. Her tattered dress was so low cut that they almost spilled out. 'What about those?'

She grabbed the open neck and pulled it down so they popped out over the top.

The stranger nodded. 'Not bad.'

'Well? How about it?'

'No.'

Delilah's face distorted in anger. 'Screw you, asshole.'

'Not in this lifetime,' Curtis countered and turned away.

The whore stomped her foot on the earthen floor and flounced off to annoy another customer.

The saloon was made up of a large false front and a canvas tent for the main building. Lanterns hung from the timber rails that held up the ceiling. There were scorch marks above them, and Curtis guessed that it wouldn't be long before the place burned to the ground.

He approached the makeshift bar, made of planks on top of barrels. The squint-eyed barkeep came over to him and said, 'What'll it be, stranger?'

'Bottle.'

'Sure,' he said and turned around to get one from a wooden box behind him. He came back and placed it on the bar. 'We don't have glasses at the moment. Or beer for that matter. Hoping they'll all come the next freight day. We ain't been open long.'

Curtis placed some money beside the bottle. 'You might want to order some more canvas too.'

26

The barkeep was puzzled. He frowned. 'What do you mean?'

'If you keep hanging your lanterns up there next to the ceiling like that, it's only a matter of time before you have a fire.'

An alarmed expression came across the man's face as he looked up. 'Oh, yes. I see what you mean. Thank you.'

The man scooped up the money from the bar and put it in his pocket. Curtis stood and waited.

'Was there something else?' the barkeep asked.

'Man puts down that much money for a bottle, he expects he might have some change coming his way.'

The barkeep opened his mouth to say something and then closed it. Instead, he reached into his pocket and pulled out some coins, and placed them on the bar.

'Could I get something to eat for that?' Curtis asked.

The man nodded. 'What would you like?'

'Whatever you got.'

'Stew?'

'That'll be fine.'

'Potatoes? Gravy?'

'Yes.'

The barkeep scooped up the money. 'Find a table and I'll bring it out directly.'

While he waited, Curtis observed four men enter the saloon. They were dressed in buckskin pants and wore cotton shirts, and had buckskin jackets to match. Each carried a Henry rifle and wore a wide-brimmed hat.

They were dressed like hunters, but something told Curtis they were anything but. The four of them bought a bottle each and then found a table not far from Curtis's. They were loud, and as much as he tried to ignore them, he couldn't help but overhear all they said.

It wasn't until he was halfway through his meal that things started to turn ugly. Delilah decided to work her wondrous charms on them to see if one would bite. As it turned out, one did. And he bit hard.

It started out harmlessly enough. Delilah came to their table, banter was swapped between them, and then one of the four men slapped her to the floor.

She cried out in pain and surprise. The man who'd struck her came from his seat and stood over her, his fists clenched.

'Hey!' shouted the barkeep. 'There's no call for that.'

The angry man glared at him. 'You shut your mouth or you'll get what she's about to.'

Curtis shook his head and eased up the Yellow Boy from where it rested against his table. He came erect, worked the lever, and a .44 Henry round slammed home into the breech.

'You owe the lady an apology, friend,' he drawled. 'Be best for all concerned if you do it now.'

The man looked at Curtis. 'Who the hell are you?' he snarled.

'It don't matter who I am. Just what I'll do if you don't apologize.'

He walked around his table and stood near the one

where the four had been seated.

'I suggest you stay out of this, friend,' said the man Curtis had pegged as the one in charge.

'Tell your boy to stand down and he might just live to finish his bottle.'

One of the other men made to lurch to his feet. 'By Christ, I. . . .'

Curtis moved with the speed of an angry rattler. The Yellow Boy suddenly reversed, and the brass butt plate hit the man between the eyes, splitting the skin wide. His legs gave beneath him and he slumped into the chair, stunned, and bright red blood poured down his face.

The weapon came back around just as the woman beater clawed at the gun on his hip. The Winchester in Curtis' grasp roared, and the slug hit its target hard in the chest. The man staggered back a few steps, shock etched on his unshaven face.

Curtis worked the lever in a fluid motion and fired again. This time the man fell across the table behind him, scattering the bottles left there by patrons who'd not long vacated it.

He moaned and rolled to the side, sliding from the table into a heap on the dirt floor.

The Yellow Boy had been loaded and moved again. This time it was an inch from the nose of the man in charge. He froze.

Curtis said in a low voice, 'I'm going back to my meal. If you have any objections, speak up. I'd much rather finish it without having to kill anyone else.'

'Kill the son of a bitch, Vince,' blurted the bleeding

man still blinded by the thick flow.

The man answered in a cool voice, 'Nope. No problem.'

Curtis lowered his weapon. 'You might want to teach your boys it ain't polite to hit a lady.'

Vince stared up at him through pale blue eyes. 'Who are you, stranger?'

'Name's Jim Curtis.'

Vince's eyes narrowed. 'Are you the one the Mexicans call El Tigre?'

'I've been called that,' Curtis said, and went back to his table.

He heard the man called Vince say, 'Murray, get Welsh outta here and then get Bell patched up.'

Curtis had only just restarted his stew when Delilah came across to his table.

'Thank you, mister,' she said in a hushed tone. 'I ain't never had a feller stand up for me like that before.'

Curtis stared at her. 'Your boss did.'

She nodded. 'Yeah, but he don't belong out here. You've seen what he's like. They would have ate him right up.'

The man known as El Tigre forked in another mouthful of potato and let his gaze linger on the whore. 'Most probably,' he agreed. 'But at least he was man enough to do it. Not like the others in this place who just watched.'

She pulled out the second chair and sat down. She waited for Curtis to say something but he remained silent.

'Did I hear you say your name was Jim?'

He paused. Ever since the death of his wife, his name being uttered from the lips of another woman always sounded funny. 'Call me Curtis.'

He kept eating while she watched, pausing only to push the bottle of whisky towards her. 'Have a drink.'

'Thank you.'

She picked up the bottle and Curtis noticed the tremor in her hand. She put the bottle back on the table, winced, and then wiped her mouth with the back of her hand.

He put the fork down, clasped his hands in front of himself, and stared at her once more.

Delilah gave him a puzzled look. 'What?'

'How come you're here? You ain't a whore. I've seen my share and you ain't nothing like them.'

'How would you know what I'm like?' she snapped.

'For starters, you still have all your teeth. Second, most whores I know that have been working on their backs tend to lose the spark in their eyes after the first year of doing it. You still have yours. And under all that grime and crap on your face, I'd wager there's a pretty lady. So, tell me, what are you doing here?'

'Long story.'

'Time is something I got plenty of.'

She remained silent for a long time. He could see her mind ticking over as she fought whether to tell him her life story or not. Then, 'I had a husband once, you know. I was married to the most wonderful man you would ever meet.'

'What happened?'

31

'He's buried on the outskirts of this hole.'

Curtis waited for her to continue.

'We were headed west to a valley where the grass is green and there's acres for the taking. We had paper for it and all. We got this far before he was killed by some man he had never seen before. Said he stole money from his saddle-bags the night before we were set to continue our journey.'

'Did he?'

Delilah looked offended. 'No! He would never do that. He didn't need to because we had over a thousand dollars of our own.'

'If you had that much money, why are you still here?'

'Because it was stolen the night my husband was killed. But no one would listen. They figured I was lying to clear his name even after he was dead.'

Curtis thought some and came to the conclusion that her husband had been killed because of the land.

'How long ago did that happen?'

'Two months.'

That's why she still had spirit.

'And you ended up with a job here as a whore.'

'I had nothing. No money and nowhere to go. When the money was taken, the papers were, too. Lester was decent enough to take me in. If nothing else, he's a sweet man. The idea of . . . of selling myself, was mine alone.'

'Where is the place you were headed?'

'Swiftcreek. It's at the foot of the mountains to the west. Many miles from here. We were told the place we were to get had grass for cattle and all the trees for lumber we would need to build our home.'

'What's your name?' Curtis asked.

'Delilah.'

'Your real name?'

She turned red. 'Mary-Alice Condon.'

Curtis smiled at her. 'Pleased to meet you, Mary-Alice.'

'Delilah! Customers waiting,' Lester called to her.

'I have to go,' she said and climbed to her feet. 'Thank you for what you did.'

El Tigre nodded and said, 'Ma'am.'

No sooner had she gone back to work when another shadow loomed over him. Curtis looked up and saw Vince.

'Mind if I sit?' he asked.

'Depends.'

'On what?'

'On whether you figure on trying to kill me for dropping your boy.'

Vince shook his head. 'Nope.'

'Take a seat then,' Curtis told him and dropped his hand under the table so it was close to the butt of the Remington.

'Fact is,' Vince said after he was seated, 'I was hoping to offer you a job since you caused me to be one man short.'

'That was his doing, not mine.'

'Granted. But it don't change the fact I'm still short a man.'

'All right,' said Curtis. 'I'm listening.'

'We're riding to join up with a feller who wants some extra hands. Got himself a lumber business in a valley loaded with tall pines. Only problem is, others were there before him and he's having trouble getting them to sell. He stands to make a fortune from the timber and he's willing to pay for it.'

Curtis thought carefully before he spoke next. 'Where is this place?'

'Swiftcreek. West of here at the foot of the mountains.'

Curtis shook his head. 'I'm headed to Abilene. This was just a stopover for me.'

'You sure? Pay's good. Five hundred a man. Shouldn't take longer than a week to sort it out.'

'Sounds to me like the feller who's doing the hiring wants more than just to buy these folks out.'

Vince's face remained passive. 'Whatever it takes.'

Curtis shook his head. 'Nope. Like I said. I'm headed to Abilene.'

Vince sighed. 'Too bad. Be seeing you around, Curtis.'

He got up from the table and couldn't resist another attempt before he left. 'You know where to find me if you change your mind.'

CHAPTER 2

'Get up. We're leaving,' Curtis said as he ripped the curtain back from the sole window of the rough-built shack.

'What?' Mary-Alice was bemused.

'I said get up.'

She sat erect in her bed, the blankets falling away to reveal her top half. She rubbed at her eyes so they would focus against the light. Beside her, another form stirred. It was Lester.

'Go away,' came the muffled voice from the face buried in the stained pillow.

'What's he doing here?' Curtis asked.

'It's his shack. We share it,' Mary-Alice paused. Then, 'Just what the hell are you doing here?'

'Get dressed and I'll explain on the way.'

'The way where?'

'To that valley you and your husband were going to.'

She flopped on to her back. 'Now I know you're full of crap.'

'Damn it,' Curtis cursed. He stepped forward to rip the covers back and exposed the two naked forms beneath them.

'Get out!' Mary-Alice screeched, and Lester rolled out of the bed and sprang to his feet. He cocked his fists, fully awake, and made to meet the threat.

He danced about and cursed, 'Come on, you son of a bitch, I'll have you.'

El Tigre shook his head. 'Get dressed before you get hurt. You might as well come too. No sense in you staying around here. You'll be out of business and dead within a month.'

Lester stared at Mary-Alice. 'Do you have any idea of what he is talking about?'

'Not one.'

Curtis bit back a curse and said, 'OK. Both of you just shut up and listen. I'll say this only once. I'm riding out of here and heading west to a place called Swiftcreek.'

Mary-Alice's eyes widened. 'That's it, you heard me right. That feller I shot yesterday was headed there with his pards. Seems they were hired to do some killing for a man who's trying to monopolize the timber.'

Lester frowned. 'What does that mean?'

'Shut up, Lester,' Curtis snapped. 'If what they say is true, then there is a good chance that your husband was murdered for the land and the papers you had on it. The money was just a bonus. Now, if you wish, you can tag along and just maybe there is a chance to get your land back. But it will be dangerous. Are you in?'

Lester said, 'No. I. . . .'

'Hell yes, I'm in,' Mary-Alice almost shouted. 'Just wait for me to get dressed.'

Curtis looked at Lester. 'You want to change your mind?'

The saloon owner's shoulders slumped. 'All right, I'll come.'

'You'll need horses and supplies. Guns and ammunition, too.'

Lester paled, 'Oh, I. . . .'

'Shut up, Lester. Just do it.'

An hour later they rode west out of Opal with Lester leading the packhorse loaded with their supplies.

'We're being followed,' said Curtis without taking his eyes off the trail ahead.

Lester turned in the saddle. 'I can't see anything.'

'They're there,' Curtis assured him.

'Who?'

'White men. At first I thought they were Indians, but they're not.'

'What will we do?' Mary-Alice asked, uncertainty in her voice.

'Let them make the first move. They're back there to our right, in the trees. They may leave us alone, but I doubt it. They've been there for the past hour.'

They kept on until dark and still the men following them remained out of sight. It wasn't until Curtis and the others were sitting around the campfire that they came in.

'I sure wish they'd do something,' Lester said as he

poked at the fire with a stick. 'This waiting will be the death of me.'

Curtis eared back the hammer on the Yellow Boy and said, 'Looks like you'll get your wish.'

'Huh?'

They came out of the darkness. Three men. The men wore fringed buckskins and fur hats. They were unshaven and filthy. Curtis figured that if the breeze had been blowing the right way he probably would have smelled them, too. Their eyes told Curtis all he needed to know.

The three men remained silent as they ran their hungry gazes over Mary-Alice.

'You fellers going to speak, or just gawk at the woman all night?'

The man who stood to the fore shifted his gaze and said, 'I'll give you twenty dollars for the woman.'

Mary-Alice gasped.

Lester came to his feet and said, 'She ain't for sale.'

'I wasn't talking to you,' the man snapped. He stared at Curtis. 'I was asking him. I mean to have her. We just need to settle on a price.'

Curtis stared at him across the fire and could see the wanton expression on his face. If they took Mary-Alice they would use her up and then kill her or sell her to the next man they came across.

'Friend, I'll give you and your pards one minute to turn your sorry asses around and get the hell out of here. After that, you'll be feeding the wolves.'

They never moved.

El Tigre nodded. 'OK. Have it your way.'

The one who spoke shifted his stare to Mary-Alice. 'Ma'am, I suggest you move away from these fellers a touch just so you're out of the way.'

Curtis was done with talk. His next move was to act. And he did so with a sudden fury.

The Yellow Boy came around with practised ease and lined up on the man. The weapon roared, and a .44 Henry slug exploded from the barrel in a flash of flame.

The man's head snapped back as the bullet smashed through his skull. He crumpled to the damp ground at his feet and didn't move.

The leader of the bunch made a move before his friend had finished falling. His right hand flashed across his body to pull a six-gun, but was barely wrapped around it by the time Curtis had levered and squeezed the trigger on the Yellow Boy again. The bullet hammered into his chest and he stumbled back until his feet got tangled and he fell.

Curtis came to his feet and worked the lever once more. The Yellow Boy came into line with the third man, and when he realized he was about to die, he abandoned all hope of drawing his gun and threw his arms in the air.

'Don't shoot!' his high-pitched scream dripped with fear. 'I ain't going for my gun.'

'You should have,' Curtis said, his voice like ice, and squeezed the trigger.

The shot rocked the night, and the man was thrust back and fell beside his friends.

Mary-Alice watched on in horrified silence at the

coldness of the man in their midst. Lester said in a high-pitched voice, 'What did you do that for? He wasn't going to shoot.'

'And maybe if I let him go he wouldn't have trailed us in the hope of getting some sort of revenge for his friends,' Curtis snarled. 'Wake up, man. This country is dangerous. Out here you can be killed every day. Make yourself useful and drag them out beyond the camp.'

Lester looked as though he was going to protest, but a glare from Curtis silenced any words in his throat.

Mary-Alice looked at him with a wide-eyed gaze. 'You killed them. All three of them.'

'Seemed like the thing to do at the time.'

Her expression hardened. 'Good. I'm pleased. They were animals.'

Curtis said to Lester, 'Take care of her. I'll be back.'

'Where are you going?'

'To find their horses. No sense in leaving them.'

Later that evening, after the others had turned in, Curtis was out beyond the firelight on watch when a noise brought him alert: Mary-Alice came out of the darkness.

'You should be asleep,' he told her as she sat beside him.

'I couldn't. Not after what happened. What makes people do things like that?' Mary-Alice asked.

He knew exactly what men would do when the circumstances were right. He'd experienced it first hand.

As a result, he'd changed. Gone was the man he'd once been. And along came 'El Tigre'. A man devoid of emotion except the one to help people in their time of need. Even if he had to kill to do it.

'It's the way some folks are,' he said. 'I've seen things that people should never have to. It's a brutal world. Maybe one day things'll get better.'

'How long before we get to Swiftcreek?'

'Another week or so.'

'Do you think it will be bad?'

'It always is.'

CHAPTER 3

'Who do you think he is?' Mary-Alice asked.

Curtis knelt beside the dead man and went through his pockets. He found nothing to identify him. All he found was a watch and a couple of dollars.

'He's been shot in the back, twice,' Curtis pointed out. 'Maybe sometime this morning.'

'Is this what you meant by trouble?' Mary-Alice asked him.

Curtis nodded. 'Let's get you both into town and I'll find out what I can about all this.'

The sound of distant hoofbeats grew louder and El Tigre turned to look. Four riders bobbed in the saddle as they appeared over a small hill to the north. He walked across to his roan and took the Yellow Boy from its scabbard.

'Do you think they mean to cause us trouble?' Lester asked.

'Never can be too careful.'

Lester reached down to draw his Henry. Curtis stopped him. 'Leave it be. I got this. You just keep an eye on Mary-Alice.'

He hesitated. 'OK.'

The riders came to a stop before them. Three men and a woman. 'Look!' the blonde-headed lady said, pointing at the body in the grass. 'He's killed Eric.'

Six-guns came clear of leather and pointed in Curtis' direction. Hammers were thumbed back and fingers whitened on triggers.

'Whoa there,' Curtis said in a loud voice. 'I ain't responsible for this.'

'You're here and you have a rifle in your hands,' a younger man accused.

'And I'll use it if you don't point them guns in another direction because this feller was dead when we got here. Shot in the back.'

'Something a coward like you would do for your boss,' the young man hissed.

'Kid,' Curtis cautioned, 'if you keep that up, I'll make you eat that gun and you'll shit bullets for a week.'

'Easy, Cody,' an older man warned him. 'Let's hear him out.'

Curtis ran his gaze over the man. He was in his fifties, had grey hair and a weathered face. The woman was in her twenties and Curtis guessed she was his daughter. The other two, Cody included, were probably around the same age.

'We just got here today,' Curtis told him. 'Found the body just like it was. Figured to ride into town and report it.'

'What's your name?'

'Curtis. Jim Curtis. This here is Mary-Alice and Lester.'

The man nodded. 'I heard of you. Killer, I'm told. But no one ever mentioned you plugging a feller in the back. So I guess maybe you don't work for Brotherton.'

'He doesn't,' Mary-Alice exclaimed. 'None of us do.'

'Is that right, missy?' the man said.

'I didn't catch your name,' Curtis pointed out.

'Morris,' the man said. 'Doug Morris. My daughter is Beth. Cody is my son, and this feller is Quint. We own this land back into the foothills. The dead man is Eric Fellows, my foreman.'

'Sounds like you know who's responsible.'

Morris nodded. 'Uh huh. Bernard Brotherton. B.B. as he likes to be called. He's trying to buy up all of the land around here, just for the timber. He's run people off a couple of times, but so far, no one has died before now. I guess it's a sign of what's to come.'

'I beg to differ,' Mary-Alice cut in.

'What's that, ma'am?'

'Someone has died before now,' she said.

'How do you know that?'

'Because it was my husband they killed.'

'Ma'am?'

'We were coming to Swiftcreek to take up land. My husband was accused of a crime and killed for it. The man responsible took all of the money we had and the papers we had for the land.'

Morris studied her. 'Do you remember where the

44

land was?'

'A small valley north of town with a creek running through it, and it backed on to a large stand of trees we were to use to build our home. Do you know it?'

Morris nodded. 'Brotherton land.'

'Ma'am,' Beth Morris interjected. 'What did the man look like? Did he have a name?'

Mary-Alice thought back and nodded. 'Ike something.'

'Ike Andrews?'

'Yes, that's it.'

'Brotherton man,' Morris said. 'I guess you're telling the truth.'

'Why would I lie?'

'Yes, why indeed?'

'I'd like to offer my services,' Curtis said unexpectedly.

'What?'

'I want a job and I'd like you to hire me.'

'Why on earth would I do that?'

Curtis said, 'Because you have more trouble coming.'

He went on to tell them about his stopover in Opal.

'They told you this?' Morris asked.

'Yeah.'

The rancher thought for a time and then shook his head. 'Nope. Hiring you would only bring us more trouble.'

'It's coming whether you like it or not. It's time to make the choice on how you want to meet it.'

'Nope,' Morris said again.

45

Curtis started to ease his horse forward. 'Come on.'

'Where are you going?' Morris snapped.

'Town.'

Swiftcreek's main street was a churned-up mess from all the heavy wagons that ran back and forth from the Brotherton Sawmill. As he rode along it, Curtis wondered why the town would stand for it when there was an alternative route around town.

Apart from the ugly scarification the town itself looked rather inviting. The false fronts on all the shops seemed new, and most of the canvas which had once extended out the back from them had been replaced with new lumber.

There were three saloons, a jail, an assayers' office, plus other amenities that were necessary for a growing town.

Curtis eased his horse to a halt outside a small false-fronted business with a shingle out front that read 'Lands Office'.

'What are we doing here?' Mary-Alice asked.

'Asking questions,' Curtis told her.

They dismounted and climbed the steps on to the rough-hewn plank boardwalk.

'I'll wait outside if you don't mind.' Lester watched as they walked towards the door.

Curtis shrugged. 'Suit yourself.'

They went inside and found a solid-looking man with dark hair behind the counter. He looked up from the work he was doing and smiled. He said, 'Good afternoon, sir, ma'am. How can I help you?'

'We're looking for some information about some land north of here that belongs to the lady,' Curtis said.

'Of course. Does the lady have the paperwork?'

Curtis shook his head. 'Nope. Her husband was killed and it was taken from him.'

His gaze flicked to Mary-Alice. 'Oh, dear. I'm very sorry, ma'am.'

She gave him a faint smile and said, 'Thank you, Mr. . . ?'

'Blake, ma'am. Terence Blake. You are?'

'Mary-Alice Condon.'

Blake nodded. 'I'm sorry, Mrs Condon, but without the papers there isn't much I can do.'

'You must have records?' Curtis said.

'Yes we . . . who are you?'

'No one special. Records?'

Blake eyed Curtis with caution. 'We do. . . .'

'Well then, check.'

Blake considered protesting, but something about this stranger told him not to. Instead, he walked across to a filing cabinet and found the paperwork for the land. He came back to the counter, read over the paper and looked up. 'Eric Condon was your husband?'

Mary-Alice nodded. 'Yes.'

Blake frowned. 'According to this the land was signed over to Bernard Brotherton.'

'That's a lie,' Mary-Alice snapped.

'It says so right here.'

Curtis reached across and snatched the form from his grasp.

'Hey!'

El Tigre ignored him and read it for himself. It was right there, true enough. But it didn't add up. Curtis knew it was fake, but it looked good enough to hold up in a court of law.

He held it across in front of Mary-Alice and pointed at the signature. In hope he asked, 'Is this your husband's mark?'

Mary-Alice studied it. She shook her head. 'I don't understand.'

'I'm sorry, ma'am,' Blake said. 'There's nothing I can do.'

Curtis looked it over once again, then something caught his eye. 'Mary-Alice, when was your husband killed?'

'Almost three months ago, on the fifteenth.'

Curtis gave a cold smile. 'This paper is dated the twenty-eighth. Someone made a mistake.'

Blake frowned. 'Give me a look.'

Curtis passed it over. 'It's right there at the bottom.'

The lands agent seemed to pale noticeably. 'Oh, my. You're right.'

'Looks like it was forged to me. There's no way a dead man could sign it.'

Blake stared at him. 'How do I know that you are telling the truth?'

'Wait here,' Curtis ordered.

He walked to the door, opened it and said to Lester, 'Get in here.'

Lester entered and Curtis said, 'Tell Blake here when Mary-Alice's husband was killed.'

There was a long silence and Lester looked at the ceiling as he calculated dates in his head. He nodded and then, 'Fifteenth.'

'Does that help?'

'Not really.'

'Lester, go and find the local law and have him come over.'

'Do I. . . .'

Curtis glared at him.

'Sure, right away.'

The former saloon owner disappeared and Blake asked Curtis, 'Just what do you intend to do.'

'Well, what you are going to do while we wait is draw up a new contract. One that stipulates that Mary-Alice is the owner.'

'I can't do that,' he blustered. 'The land belongs to Mr Brotherton.'

'No, it don't.'

They were still arguing the finer points a few minutes later when Sheriff Clem Smith entered. He was a portly man but had an element of toughness about him.

'What's going on, Blake?' he growled.

Blake told him and the sheriff shifted his gaze to Curtis. 'Who are you?'

'Jim Curtis.'

His face remained passive. 'The feller they call El Tigre?'

'Maybe.'

He nodded. 'Hand over the paper, Blake.'

Smith looked it over and asked some more questions.

'How do I know what you are saying is the truth?'

'The feller who killed her husband goes by the name of Ike Andrews.'

'Now that don't surprise me. What are your intentions, ma'am?' he asked Mary-Alice.

'I want what is rightfully mine.'

'It'll have to go to court,' the sheriff said. 'Mind you, it looks as though you have a good case. However, I don't like your chances.'

'Why?'

'Let's just say that the judge and Brotherton are kinda friendly.'

'You mean he's in this Brotherton's pocket?' Mary-Alice stated.

'Yes, ma'am.'

Curtis took the paper and stared at Smith. 'How about you?'

The lawman gave him an indignant look. 'I'll pretend I didn't hear that.'

'OK. You're not. Mr Blake, is this the only copy of this paper?'

'As far as I know.'

'Good,' Curtis said, and tore it up.

'You can't do that!' the lands man exclaimed.

Smith chuckled.

'Draw up another paper, Blake. One that states that Mary-Alice Condon owns the land. Like I asked you before.'

'I've got to hand it to you, Curtis. You think on your feet. You figure that this might swing things the woman's way when the only piece of paper declares

50

her the owner?'

'What it does is set things right.'

'You know he won't stand for it. He won't back away from it.'

'Neither will I,' Curtis declared. He shifted his gaze to Mary-Alice. 'This will get bad before it gets better. More than likely men will die. It's up to you.'

She said, 'Even if I get it, I don't have any money to do anything.'

Curtis reached into his pocket and pulled out a wad of money. He held it out. 'There's close to a thousand dollars there – take it.'

Mary-Alice looked horrified. 'I can't take it.'

'Yeah, you can. I can get more. Lester and I can build you a cabin until something better can be afforded. With all the lumber on your land it shouldn't be a problem. You can stock the range with young cattle, too.'

'And where would I get them from?'

'I'll see Doug Morris. See if we can come to an arrangement.'

'If we live long enough,' Lester put in.

Curtis ignored him. 'Well?'

Mary-Alice nodded. 'Let's do it.'

El Tigre looked at Smith. 'You got any objection?'

'Nope. Should be downright interesting.'

'What should be?'

They all turned and stared at the man who filled the doorway.

CHAPTER 4

He was a solid-looking man in his forties, dressed in ranch-hand's clothes, and he wore a Colt Army on his hip. His face was weathered, and his deep voice had an air of authority about it.

'Yep,' Smith said, 'should be interesting.'

'Would someone like to tell me what is going on?'

'This, ladies and gents, is Bernard Brotherton,' Smith said.

'Bernard, meet Lester, Curtis, and Mary-Alice Condon.'

The last name was spoken for effect but there was no sign of any.

'Pleased to meet you all. If you're here looking to buy land, there's not much left, I'm afraid. By the way, call me B.B.'

'We don't need to buy it. The lady already owns some.'

Brotherton was confused. 'She does?'

'Yeah, north of town.'

'I'm sorry, but I own all the holdings north of town.'

52

'No, you think you do.'

Brotherton switched his gaze. 'Mr Blake, would you care to explain.'

'I . . . ahh. . . .'

Curtis said, 'You thought you owned the land, Brotherton. But someone messed up. You see, when you get a man to sign the papers you might want to make sure he hasn't been dead for two weeks already.'

Brotherton stared at Curtis. It was a fool mistake and he knew it. But he didn't want to make too much of it just in case it wound up in court. Not that it would matter with Judge Reed, but courts drew attention. No, better to just wait and kill them after. He wasn't about to pass up all that timber on the land. Unless. . . .

'What are your intentions, Mrs Condon?' he asked tightly.

'We intend to settle on the land.'

'How about I save you some trouble and make an offer for the land instead?'

Mary-Alice hesitated. 'I . . . I don't think so.'

Brotherton shrugged his shoulders and said, 'Oh, well. Enjoy your stay.'

And then he left.

After the door closed, Smith frowned. 'That was way too easy.'

'I agree,' said Curtis. 'He'll leave it up to Vince and his men.'

'Who's Vince?' the sheriff asked.

Curtis said, 'Hired gun. Asked me if I wanted to join them. Told him no.'

'That's all I need,' Smith said. 'More guns.'

'You won't get any trouble out of me, Sheriff. Not unless it comes calling.'

'Yeah, that's what worries me.'

They made the decision to spend the night in town. The following morning, Curtis would escort them to the valley where the land was, and then he would go and see Morris about some cattle.

Curtis left them at the hotel for the evening. He decided to enjoy a few drinks at one of the saloons, and chose the Silver Aspen. He bought a bottle and found a battered table in the corner. While he was seated there, he saw Brotherton come in, walk across to the biggest man at the bar, say something in his ear, then leave. At that point, Curtis wondered what had happened to Vince and his men. He was certain they would have made it here before him.

The man at the bar moved towards his table, his gaze not wavering from Curtis as he approached.

So, this is how it's going to be.

The man stopped in front of Curtis and stared at him in menacing silence.

'Apache war party cut out your tongue?' Curtis asked.

'Huh?'

'Speak or get out!'

That got the ball started. He snarled something incoherent and grasped the front edge of the table. With a mighty sweep of his arm, the table flew to the left, scattering Curtis's bottle and glass.

His jaw dropped when he saw that Curtis had drawn the Remington from its holster and had it pointing straight at him. Without hesitation, El Tigre squeezed the trigger and the six-gun discharged. The slug exploded from the barrel and crashed into the bull's chest.

He staggered backwards, and Curtis shot him twice more with a brutal coldness that stunned those who witnessed it.

The man sank to his knees and fell on to his side. Curtis came to his feet and scanned the room for any other threats that Brotherton may have left in his wake.

'That was blasted murder!' a thin-faced man exclaimed.

Curtis stared him in the eye and shook his head. 'Nope, that was killing.'

The batwings flew open and Brotherton entered. Vince was beside him. Curtis saw him and said, 'You took your time getting here.'

He remained silent.

Brotherton looked shocked by the sight of the dead man on the floor. He glanced at Curtis and back to Vince. 'You know him?'

Vince nodded. 'Surprised to see you here.'

El Tigre shrugged. 'Took the long way.'

'You had no intention of going to Abilene, did you?'

'I did, but I talked to a feller and he convinced me otherwise.'

It was then that Sheriff Smith chose to appear. He

took one look at the man on the floor and asked, 'What happened.'

'It was murder, Clem,' the thin-faced man blurted out. 'Bremmer didn't even have a gun.'

Smith stared at Curtis and waited for him to speak. Curtis said, 'That was his mistake. Thought he could tear me apart without one.'

'So, you shot him?' Smith asked.

'Have you seen the size of him? The bastard was the size of a bull buffalo.'

'Arrest him, Smith,' Brotherton snapped. 'You heard the man, it was murder.'

Smith glared at Brotherton and Curtis said, 'Fine. Arrest me. But first, give me the chance to shoot this asshole for putting his man on to me.'

'I what?'

'I saw you come in and talk to him. Seems mighty strange that your man would then come over to my table and start something he couldn't finish.'

'You can't prove anything.'

Curtis raised the Remington until it was pointed at Brotherton's guts. He eared back the hammer and said in a cool voice, 'Vince, get your boss out of here before I gutshoot him.'

It was obvious Brotherton had never been threatened like this before, and didn't like it one bit. Curtis watched them go and looked at Smith.

The sheriff said, 'You just pissed against the wrong tree, my friend.'

'He started it. But if he wants to push me, I'll sure as hell finish it.'

*

'It's beautiful,' Mary-Alice gasped as she looked around at the vista which was her new home.

'It sure is something,' Curtis agreed.

As far as the eye could see was a carpet of lush green set against a backdrop of large pines. No wonder Brotherton wanted the land.

Curtis eased his roan over to the creek and stared down into its crystal clearness at the round rocks scattered along the bottom of it. He climbed down and took a knee beside the water and scooped out a handful. He put it to his lips and tasted it. The liquid was cool and sweet. Spring fed from further up the valley, no doubt.

He was just about to climb back to his feet when he saw it.

Curtis' blood ran cold as he stared at the massive paw print in the soft ground beside the creek. He opened his hand as far as it would go and placed it down. It didn't even touch the sides. Somewhere out there was one hell of a big bear.

El Tigre finally stood erect and looked around. He glanced across at the others and said, 'Don't wander off.'

Lester took on a nervous expression. 'What is it?'

'Bear sign.'

Lester's head pivoted so fast that it seemed as though it might come loose. 'Where?'

Curtis pointed to it. Lester swallowed hard. 'I think we should go back to town, now.'

57

'Don't worry. He's probably long gone. They like to keep on the move.'

'I hope you're right.'

Curtis stared at Mary-Alice. He said, 'I'm going to take a ride over to Morris' tomorrow and have a word to him. Hopefully purchase that bull and some cows to start a herd.'

'But I don't think I have enough money for that,' Mary-Alice pointed out.

'I do. It'll be fine.'

She shook her head. 'No. I couldn't ask you to do that.'

'All right, how about I put up the money for a fifty per cent stake in the place,' he saw her face change and knew she was about to protest. He held up a hand and added, 'Before you get all het up about it, think on this. Once the place is up and running and making you money, you then can buy me out for the exact amount that I put into it.'

Mary-Alice hesitated, and then relented and said, 'OK. We'll do it that way.'

CHAPTER 5

One month later

The month that followed was quiet but busy. With hired help, the house was built along with a bunkhouse, barn and corrals. Morris sold Curtis a bull and twenty head of cattle. The start of a herd. He then bought a couple of horses and found a rundown wagon in town which he bought and fixed up. It had been the longest he'd ever stayed in one place for quite a spell.

Mary-Alice was happy, happier than she'd been in a while, and it was obvious. Lester found himself a new calling as a cowhand and took particular pride in learning all that he could about the ones that were on the land.

But that was all about to change.

Brotherton looked up at Vince from behind his desk. 'It's time to do something.'

The killer nodded. 'Good. All this sitting around ain't good for a man. What do you have in mind?'

'To move forward we're going to need a free hand. To get it, we'll need the sheriff out of the way.'

Vince nodded. 'OK. We can take care of that. We'll do it tonight.'

'Good. I have a man lined up to come in and take over as sheriff. I also want you to shoot that woman's cattle.'

Vince knew who he meant. 'Just the cattle? What about Curtis?'

'No. Just give them a warning.'

'I'll tell you now, he ain't the type to take warnings to heart.'

'We'll see,' Brotherton said. 'That leaves Morris. I've had enough of side-stepping around him. I want that timber on his land. With him out of the way, Cody will sell the timber stands to me.'

'You sound like that's possible,' Ike Andrews observed from the corner.

'A little bird told me that Morris split the ranch between both of his kids in his will. I've had a chat to young Cody and he's all for selling the timber rights to me after his father is gone.'

'You mean he's more or less said that he don't care if we kill his old man?'

'He's looking upon the gains he can make with his father out of the way.'

Surprised, Andrews said, 'All right then. I'll take care of it.'

'You don't have to, he's going to do it himself.'

Andrews let out a low whistle. 'There's a son who loves his father.'

'Loves his father's money more.'

Vince asked, 'Who's the feller you got coming in to take over the badge?' Vince asked.

'Reynolds.'

There was no need to say anything else.

Sheriff Smith walked slowly along the boardwalk. He stopped occasionally to peer into darkened store windows to check all was well. It wasn't long after midnight and he was on his last round before going to bed for the night.

He stepped down from the boardwalk, crossed the mouth of one of Swiftcreek's many alleys, and then up the steps on the other side.

When his boots hit the top he paused. A noise had emanated from the alley he'd just passed. Smith turned back and stared into the gloom.

The sheriff frowned and walked back down the steps. Then he moved a few yards into the alley. 'Hello, anyone there?'

His words were met with silence. Another couple of steps and he stopped again. 'Hello?'

The alley exploded with the crash of gunfire. Three bullets slammed into Smith's chest and made him stagger back. His jaw dropped in shock and he tried to draw breath into his shattered lungs.

The sheriff dropped to his knees and then tipped on to his side. As he died the town was just coming to life to see what the noise was all about.

The sound brought Curtis awake. At first, he wasn't

sure what it was. It was too far away for him to be certain. But as he came fully awake it suddenly dawned on him what it was. Gunshots!

'Damn it!' he snarled and came to his feet. 'Lester, get up!'

His shout was met with a groan.

'Get up, damn it!'

Lester groaned again. 'Why?'

'I think someone is shooting our cattle.'

Lester flew up in his cot. 'What? Why? How do you know?'

'It's about the only reason I can think of why someone is shooting at this time of night,' Curtis said as he dragged his pants on.

Before Curtis hit the door, Lester was dressed. El Tigre scooped up the Yellow Boy and ran out the door.

Out in the yard, Curtis stopped and listened. Clearer now, the gunfire was coming from the east. Now he was even more certain they were shooting the cattle because that's where they were.

'Get the horses,' Curtis snapped.

Lester ran over to the corral and fought to get the horses ready while Curtis ran across to the main house. He banged on the door and it was answered almost immediately by Mary-Alice.

'What's going on?' she asked. 'Is that shooting?'

'Yes, stay here. We'll go and check it out.'

'Be careful.'

He turned away and rushed across to the corral. Lester said, 'We don't have saddles. It was quicker that way.'

62

'Don't matter. Let's go.'

They thundered out of the yard and headed east across the lush green pasture painted silver by the large, full moon overhead. It made the landscape brighter and easier to navigate obstacles.

A mile from the house the pasture lifted and the horses raced up a gentle slope. When they topped the rise they reined in.

'There!' Lester exclaimed. 'I can see them.'

So could Curtis. There were two men riding amidst what remained of the cattle. The cows were scattered which made it harder for them to finish off all of them.

'Son of a bitch,' Curtis hissed and brought up his Winchester. From this distance in the light which the moon provided, there was no way he could be sure of hitting anyone. But he sure as hell meant to try.

After the first shot crashed out, El Tigre levered in a fresh round and fired again. He did that another three times before heeling his roan forward. 'Come on, Lester. Let's run these bastards off.'

They rode hard down the other side of the slope towards the nightriders. One of them saw Curtis and Lester coming and shouted to his friends. They whirled their horses about and galloped away.

Curtis and Lester reined in when they reached the dead animals. Lester called across to Curtis, 'What are we stopping for?'

'We won't catch them now.'

Lester looked around at the scattered lumps in the grass. 'Why did they do this?'

'It was a warning.'

'Who . . . Brotherton? Brotherton did this?'

'More than likely ordered it done. I figure he doesn't get his hands dirty unless he has to.'

'Damn him,' Lester cursed.

'Well, looks like the peace and quiet is over.'

A loud bellow split the night.

'Sounds like that bull is still alive,' Lester commented. 'At least they didn't get him.'

'That's something. Head back to the house and tell Mary-Alice what happened. I'll stay out here and look around. Try and work out how many they killed.'

'You sure?'

'Yeah.'

'All right then. I'll see you when you get back.'

When Curtis arrived back at the ranch house shortly after first light, he brought with him bad news. There were only four cows left and the bull. The rest were dead or had to be shot because they were beyond help.

Mary-Alice was devastated at the loss. 'What are we going to do?'

'I'll ride over to Morris' spread tomorrow and see if I can arrange to get some more cattle. I've enough spare money so you should be able to get some more. Meanwhile, I've been thinking about that timber that Brotherton wants so bad.'

'What about it?' asked Lester.

'Sell some of it.'

'What?' Lester blurted out. 'Sell it?'

'I'm not selling to Brotherton,' growled Mary-Alice.

'You won't have to. There's a logging company over in Barrett, we could send them a wire.'

'But that's fifty miles away,' Mary-Alice pointed out.

'Yes, but I heard in town that they're cutting trees for ties needed by the railroad. I'd say that's what Brotherton wants the timber for. He would make a fortune if he had all of the timber sown up.'

Mary-Alice looked uncertain. 'If you're sure.'

'It may be the only choice you have. While I'm in town I'll have a talk with Smith and tell him what happened.'

'I don't think it's wise for you to go to town at all,' Mary-Alice said.

'I'll be fine.'

'It's not you I'm worried about.'

CHAPTER 6

The moment Curtis rode into Swiftcreek he could sense something was wrong. The town seemed to have lost its spark.

He eased his roan to the hitch rail outside the jail and climbed the steps on to the boardwalk. He crossed to the door and tried to open it, but found it locked. He shrugged and looked about on the off chance he could see Smith anywhere. Instead, he was met with furtive glances from townsfolk who walked by.

Curtis shrugged his shoulders and guessed it was because of who he was. He decided to come back later and stepped back down onto the street and untied the horse's reins. He led it along the street until he found the telegraph office. He hitched the horse and went inside.

The telegrapher was a thin man with light-colored hair and was in the process of writing out a message which was coming over the wire. 'Be with you in a moment.'

While he waited, Curtis glanced at some of the flyers on the wall of the office. One in particular caught his eye. It was an advertisement looking for men to cut trees, with a starting date of a week from that day. Curtis frowned. It looked to be recent.

It was signed B.B.

'What can I do for you?' the telegrapher asked.

Curtis pointed at the flyer. 'This new?'

'Went up this morning.'

'Brotherton?'

'Yes. You after work?'

'Nope. I want to send a wire.'

'Of course.'

The telegrapher gave him a stub and paper. 'Write out what you want sent. You can write?'

Curtis nodded and wrote out the message. He passed it over to the telegrapher who read it, growing paler the more he read.

'Is there a problem?' Curtis asked.

'Ahh – no. No, it . . . do you really want this sent?'

'I do. I'll wait for a reply.'

'OK.'

It took thirty minutes for the reply to come back. When Curtis read it, he smiled. Then he glared at the telegrapher. 'If this gets back to Brotherton, I'll know where it came from.'

He said nothing.

'Now, where might I find Sheriff Smith? His office was locked up.'

The man opened his mouth to speak but then it snapped shut.

Curtis frowned. 'What?'

'He's dead. He was killed last night while he was

doing his rounds.'

The news of the sheriff's death hit Curtis harder than he let on. So, this is it. Brotherton is going all in.

'Did they get who did it?'

'No.'

'So who's taken over his job? I had some trouble last night and I need to report it.'

'No one yet. I sent word today. There's a feller coming from Dobytown. I sent a wire to Fort Kearny.'

'Who? What's the feller's name?' Curtis asked.

The telegrapher gave him a knowing smile and Curtis said, 'I get it. I guess I'll just have to wait and see.'

As Curtis rode back along the street he thought about what had happened so far. The nightriders who'd killed the cows, and then someone had killed the sheriff. He had no doubt the two were connected and that Brotherton was involved. He was almost as certain that the new sheriff would be on Brotherton's payroll too. Which meant that B.B. was playing with a stacked deck.

With his plan in place, Brotherton would move on the lands he wanted. The ones that were loaded with trees. That meant Mary-Alice and the Morrises.

Ahead on the boardwalk, outside the Silver Aspen saloon, he saw two familiar faces. Murray and Bell. Vince's men.

Curtis angled his horse towards them and came to a halt. He rested his hand on the butt of his Remington and said, 'Where's your boss?'

They looked at each other and shrugged. Bell ran a hand across his stubbled chin and said, 'Not real sure.

68

Ain't seen him in a while.'

Nodding, Curtis said, 'I ain't surprised. All you fellers must've had a late night, huh?'

Murray's eyes narrowed. 'What do you mean?'

'Well, you were out our way shooting our cattle. Someone shot the sheriff. Yep, pretty busy night.'

'Don't know what you're talking about.'

'Uh, huh. Well then, let me speak real plain so dumb assholes like you fellers can understand me. The next time any of you comes on to our range, I'll put a .44 Henry slug in his hide.'

'You going to be able to back them words up, Curtis?' Bell hissed.

'You know I can.'

Bell moved away from Murray to get a clear line of sight on Curtis. 'I owe you, you son of a bitch.'

'You want to do this now?' Curtis asked. 'Here on the street with all these people around?'

'I don't care about no people,' Bell sneered.

A surge of adrenalin coursed through El Tigre's veins. For it was him now, not Curtis who faced down Bell. It was always him.

The flicker in Bell's eyes gave his intentions away. His shoulder dipped when his hand streaked towards his holstered six-gun. But El Tigre's Remington was already clear of leather and the first shot crashed out.

Bell was hit hard when the bullet smashed into his chest. He staggered, then tried to right himself. Instead, his legs gave out and he fell to the dusty street.

Curtis kicked his horse and it lunged forwards a couple of strides. Just enough to do two things. First, it helped throw off Murray's aim, and the bullet from the killer's gun flew wide of its intended mark. And second, it cleared Curtis's line of fire.

The Remington barked again, and this time Murray felt the burning pain of the slug which tore into his chest. Curtis shot him twice more for good measure.

What happened next, however, was unexpected. From further along the street a gun roared, and the bullet cut through the air close to Curtis's face.

Looking up he saw the shooter. Curtis figured he was one of Brotherton's men. He rammed the Remington back into its holster and brought the Yellow Boy free of its scabbard.

Curtis levered a round into the breech and dropped the front sight on to the figure along the street. Ahead of the weapon, people started to scatter, some even cut across his front and made his shot even harder.

Ignoring the next round which passed even closer, Curtis let out an even breath and squeezed the trigger.

He saw the puff of dust from the clothing of the shooter when the bullet struck home. The man collapsed and arched his back before lying still. Curtis levered in another round and waited in silence. His horse beneath him stood stock still.

Vince and Brotherton appeared from inside the saloon. It was Vince who spoke after he took a moment to survey the scene. His icy gaze settled on the rider on the red roan. 'What the hell happened, Curtis?'

'Your man Bell decided to try his luck. He lost.'

'Murray?'

'Dealt himself in on a losing hand. There's another feller along the street decided to do the same thing.'

Brotherton glanced to his left and saw a small crowd gathered on the street. He turned his hot glare on Curtis. 'You killed all three?'

'Yeah.'

'What are you going to do about it, Vince?'

Curtis tensed. He said, 'I think Vince did enough last night. Hit our place, killed most of our cows. Then I hear someone killed Smith. No prizes for guessing who that was.'

Vince's face remained passive.

'Vince?'

'There'll come a time,' Vince said. 'This ain't it.'

'Are you scared of him?' Brotherton asked trying to goad him into doing something.

Curtis stared hard at the man. 'He ain't scared, Brotherton. Just wise. You could learn something from him.'

Brotherton cursed out loud and stomped away. Curtis stared at Vince. 'What happened last night was like declaring war, Vince. Run off and shoot our stock. Kill the sheriff. What's next?'

'Don't know what you're talking about.'

'Understand this. I'll kill any man who Brotherton sends on to Mary-Alice's land. Killing is something I know. Something I'm good at. You might want to make sure that the feller that Brotherton brings in to be sheriff knows that too.'

Vince nodded. 'I'll do that.'

CHAPTER 7

The news out at the Morris spread didn't get any better. When Curtis rode into the ranch yard just after noon all the hands seemed to be milling about aimlessly. Like they were waiting for something to happen.

They stared and watched Curtis ride in. One of them stepped forward and asked, 'What do you want here, Curtis?'

'I came to see your boss. Is he about?'

'Mr Morris is dead. He was killed last evening while he was out riding the range.'

The news stunned Curtis. This really was bad. 'What happened?'

The man shook his head. 'One of the hands found him.'

'How are his son and daughter taking it.'

On cue, the door to the ranch house crashed open and Cody stormed out. 'Cody! Come back here!'

He ignored her and kept going.

Then Beth appeared in the doorway. 'Cody, you can't. Pa has only just been killed and this is what you do.'

Cody stopped and whirled about. 'We need the damned money, Beth. Pa couldn't see it, but I can. It's the only way.'

'What? To sell our timber to Brotherton? There are others.'

Curtis frowned. It seemed to him that the decision had been made awful quick.

'Not here there isn't.'

'I won't sign,' she said defiantly.

'I don't care. Now that Pa is gone, I run the place.'

'He said he left it to both of us.'

'There's no way a woman can run a ranch.'

'I could run it better than you. But you don't care, do you? Now that Pa is dead you think you can do things your way. Well, I'm telling you that it isn't going to happen that way.'

He started to stalk back towards her. The anger with his sister seemed to permeate from him. He placed one foot on the veranda and Curtis' voice stopped him cold. 'Think about your next move, kid.'

Cody turned to face him. 'What the hell are you doing out here?'

'Came to see your father,' Curtis explained. 'Sorry for your loss.'

'Well, now you know, get the hell off of my land.'

'Came to see if I could buy some more cows from you.'

'No!'

Beth said, 'You want to buy more? I thought you had all you wanted?'

'Nightriders rode on to the spread last night and

shot most of them.'

'Oh, no,' Beth gasped. 'Of course you can have some more.'

'I said no,' Cody snapped. 'Now get gone.'

Curtis set his jaw firm and said in a low voice, 'This ain't none of my business, but if you go and sell your timber to Brotherton it means he wins.'

Cody snarled. 'You're right. It ain't none of your business.'

'You do realize that Brotherton is behind all of this, don't you?'

'Behind what?'

'Your pa's death, the cows being shot, Sheriff Smith being killed last night.'

'What?' Beth seemed startled. 'Not Clem?'

One of the hands cursed.

Curtis nodded. 'I'd have thought you would have known. Didn't anyone go to town to report your father's death? Brotherton already has a man coming in to fill his position.'

'You can't prove that,' Cody sneered.

'It all makes sense. The one thing he wants is the timber. With your pa and Smith out of the way, he's setting himself up to get it. Shooting the cows on Mary-Alice's land last night was a warning. I guess your pa got all the warnings Brotherton was willing to give him. But you do what you want to do. Me, I aim to fight.'

'What about his hired guns?' Beth asked.

'He's three less, now,' Curtis told her. 'I killed them this morning.'

A murmur ran through the hands.

Curtis continued. 'And your sister is right, Cody. There are other options for your timber. There's a feller who'll be here in a few days to look over the stuff on Mary-Alice's spread.'

Cody shook his head. 'Ain't going to happen. Now I already told you once, but I'll tell you again, get the hell off my land.'

Curtis shrugged and made to turn his horse.

'Wait,' called Beth. 'I want to talk to you.'

Her brother glared at her, then shook his head. Then instead of rebuking her, he turned and crossed the yard to a saddled horse, climbed aboard, and rode out of the yard.

Beth called to one of the hands, 'Sam, take Mr Curtis' horse and look after it. Come inside, Mr. Curtis.'

'Would you care for a coffee?' Beth asked him as he sat at the large wooden table in the kitchen.

'I'll be fine thanks, ma'am.'

'Call me Beth.'

'Call me Jim then.'

'Fine.'

'I really am sorry about your pa,' Curtis said. 'I probably shouldn't be here.'

'No, it's fine. I've done my crying for the moment. And to answer your earlier question, Cody didn't send anyone after the sheriff because he said he'd handle it.'

Curtis nodded. 'What did you want to talk to me about?'

'About the timber and the cows.'

'What about them?'

'Tell me about the man from the company you say is coming in.'

He shrugged. 'Not much to tell. He'll be here in a few days. They cut trees to convert into rail ties.'

'Which is what Brotherton wants to do,' Beth pointed out.

'The feller that's coming will offer a lot more than Brotherton.'

'Do you think you could persuade him to come over here and talk to my brother?'

'I think your brother already has his mind made up on what he wants to do,' Curtis said.

'He can't sell anything without my signature. I know that for a fact. Pa told me when he drew up the will with his lawyer a couple of years ago.'

'Your brother strikes me as one who won't give up easy.'

She nodded.

'Does he have to sign off on selling cows to me?' Curtis asked.

'Yes,' Beth answered. 'But that is why I'll give you thirty head instead of selling them to you. We've got some young unbranded stuff that I'll get a couple of the hands to bring over to your spread.'

'Your brother will like that.'

She gave Curtis a sly smile. 'He won't even know.'

'One more thing,' he said. 'Could you get one of your hands to show me where your pa was killed?'

Beth hesitated before asking, 'Why?'

'Let's just say that you're doing something for me, so I'd like to repay the kindness. Besides, I doubt the new sheriff will be all that willing to get to the truth of the matter if he works for Brotherton.'

'You'd do that?'

'Uh huh.'

'When you go out to get your horse, tell Sam to show you. Be careful, though, Jim. Whoever shot Pa did it in his back.'

'I'll be careful.'

'He was found around here,' Sam said. The big cowhand indicated towards a large rock surrounded by grass and trees.

From where he was, Curtis could see a wide swathe of valley to his east and south. To the west was a large tract of pines. And to the north was more of the same.

'Who found him?'

'Cody did. Mr Morris had been shot in the back. Cody brought him in draped over his horse.'

'And it was normal for your boss to go out riding of an evening?'

'Sure. He used to say it was the best part of the day.'

'Only this time he never came home? Well, not alive, anyway.'

Sam nodded. 'We set out looking for him this morning. Cody told us all where to look and we rode out. It just happened that he was the one who found his pa. You be right now?'

Curtis nodded. 'Yeah.'

Sam left, and Curtis looked around. First, he found

where Morris had been shot, made visible by the blood on the ground. Then Curtis walked slow circles until he found where the bushwhacker had shot from.

Whoever it was, rode in from the same way he and Sam had done. Almost exactly, except for one difference. They'd pulled off to the side into the trees and walked closer on foot until they were sure they couldn't miss.

Which meant that they knew where they were going and where Morris would be. Curtis frowned. The killer knew his quarry. Knew his movements. He doubted that Brotherton or any of his hired killers knew Morris that well. That meant it was someone from Morris's own spread who was more than likely responsible.

But who?

Then it caught his eye. One clear shoe print. Curtis knelt and examined it. He smiled. There was a small nick in the shoe. Just a slight imperfection. At least now he knew what to look for.

John Tinkler had been Morris' lawyer for five years. The thick-set man who came west from St Louis to practise law on the frontier was stunned when Cody Morris told him that his father had been killed the previous evening.

But not as stunned as when Cody asked him for his father's will.

'I'm sorry, Cody, I can't give it to you. Your sister has to be present for the reading. Besides, your pa has only just died. Surely you'd like to wait a couple of days before we get into the particulars of his will?'

78

'I ain't waiting for nothing,' Cody told him. 'Get the damned thing like I asked.'

Tinkler shook his head. 'I'm sorry. Not without your sister present.'

Cody pulled his six-gun from leather and eared back the hammer. The lawyer paled. 'What are you doing, Cody?'

'Asking nicely.'

There was something in Cody's eyes that told the lawyer that he'd shoot him if he tried to stall again. Instead, Tinkler nodded. 'All right. But what you're doing is against the law.'

'So, tell the sheriff.'

Tinkler opened the top drawer of a cabinet against the far wall and riffled through some papers until he found what he wanted. He took it out and passed it to Cody. 'Here.'

Cody snatched the paper and read it. He gave a mirthless smile and then shook his head. 'That old bastard.'

'I guess he thought more of your sister than you,' Tinkler said. 'After this, I'm not surprised.'

Cody's eyes flared. 'He left it all to Beth.'

Tinkler nodded. 'He changed it a month ago when the trouble with Brotherton got serious and his foreman was shot.'

'Who else knows about this?'

'At this point, just you and I.'

'Good, let's keep it that way,' Cody snarled and shot Tinkler in the chest. Then he slipped out the back door before anyone could arrive.

Brotherton hadn't expected to see Cody Morris so soon. He was happy to hear the news he brought with him, however.

'Move your men on whenever you like,' Cody told him. 'After you've paid the five thousand you said you would.'

The smile on Brotherton's face said it all. 'Of course. We can go across to the bank now if you wish, and I'll withdraw it. Just sign this paper.'

Brotherton laid it out on his desk for Cody to sign. A minute later it was all done.

'Good. Let's go.'

Before they could walk out of Brotherton's well lit office the door swung open and Ike Andrews walked in. 'Someone just shot Tinkler, the lawyer.'

'Do they know who it was?' Brotherton asked.

'Nope,' Andrews said, then shifted his gaze to Cody. 'He's your pa's lawyer ain't he?'

'Was. My pa is dead.'

'Someone said they saw you going in there earlier.'

There was a flicker in Cody's eyes. Not much of one, but it gave it all away.

'It was you,' Andrews words were a statement, not a question. 'Why did you shoot him?'

'Because he was the only one who knew,' Cody explained.

'Knew what?' asked Brotherton.

'That my father left everything to Beth.'

Brotherton's eyes flared. 'What? And you stand

here ready to take my money for something you don't own?'

'It don't matter. I have the will, and I shot the only other person who knows.'

'He ain't dead,' Andrews told him. 'They carried him over to the sawbones. He's not good, but he's still hanging in there.'

Cody paled. 'Christ.'

'Looks like you have some unfinished business,' Brotherton pointed out. 'You don't get a cent until the damned lawyer is gone.'

'What does it matter. I have the will. He can't prove anything.'

'He can tell them it was you who shot him, idiot,' Andrews snapped.

'That's right,' Brotherton said. 'Get it sorted.'

'All right. I'll fix it. But there's something else you should know. There's another man coming in on the stage in a couple of days. You might say he's your competition. Going to buy timber from that woman who came in with Curtis. That way you can't get it.'

Brotherton's face set like granite. 'We'll see about that.'

When Curtis arrived back late that afternoon he broke the news to Mary-Alice and Lester about what had happened. The deaths of Morris and Smith, and about the gunfight, also how he'd offered to help Beth Morris find the killer of her father.

'What about this place?' Mary-Alice asked.

'I can do both.'

81

Mary-Alice placed a plate of stew on the table in front of where Curtis sat. 'Uh huh. Did you hear back about the wire?'

Curtis nodded 'Feller will be here in a couple of days. His name is Myers. Offering ten thousand dollars per section.'

Mary-Alice's jaw dropped. 'That much?'

'Yep.'

'How big is a section?'

'I'm not sure, but with all this timber on your land I'd say you have at least a couple.'

'So that would be twenty thousand?'

'Pretty much. That'll tide you over until you get a herd built up.'

'Oh, God yes.'

Her eyes started to leak tears. Curtis asked, 'Are you OK?'

She nodded. 'I . . . I just wish Eric was here.'

Curtis glanced across at Lester. After a slow start, the man was starting to grow on Curtis, and he could see the hurt on his face. It was quite obvious that the ex-barman had grown quite attached to Mary-Alice, but her words had hurt him.

He excused himself from the table.

'But you haven't eaten,' Mary-Alice said.

'I don't feel well. Sorry.'

After he'd gone, Mary-Alice said, 'What's wrong with him?'

Sighing, Curtis said, 'You and him need to have a talk.'

'What about?'

'About you and him.'

She frowned and then raised her eyebrows when she realized what he meant. 'Oh. You mean. . . ?'

'Yeah. He likes you. Has done for quite a spell. Don't tell me you ain't noticed?'

'I thought it was more to do with the arrangement we had in Opal.'

'It may have started out that way, but it ain't any more. Why do you think he's been working so hard around here? He's turned into quite a cowhand.'

There was concern on her face. 'Oh, my. I'm not ready for anything like that. Not yet.'

'Not yet, or not with him?'

'I don't know.'

'Well, either way, you'd best have that talk with him or things are only going to get worse around here, and there's enough going on without that.'

CHAPTER 8

Light shone from the window of the doctor's office and out across the boardwalk on to the street. Cody stood in the shadows waiting for it to go out. It was some time after midnight and the old buzzard was still awake.

'He can tell them it was you who shot him, idiot,' Andrews' voice echoed through the young man's head.

'I'll show you who's an idiot.'

He should have been back out at the ranch, but he needed to tidy this thing up or he'd not see a cent of the money Brotherton was offering.

It was another hour before the doctor's light went out, and another twenty minutes before Cody drew enough courage to try the front door. When it opened without any noise, he drew in a calming breath and stepped inside. His first step made a floorboard squeak and he froze, his ears straining against the silence to hear more than his heart beating.

When nothing moved, he kept on until he found

the room where the barely alive lawyer was sleeping. He slipped into the room and stood beside him, listening.

Every breath seemed shallow and held a rattle deep down. He sounded more dead than alive and would most likely die, but Cody couldn't take that chance.

He crossed to the bed and took the pillow from under his head. Tinkler didn't move. Cody hesitated, then placed the pillow over the lawyer's face and held it there. At the last, the dying man stiffened weakly and then relaxed. When Cody removed the pillow, Tinkler made no sound at all.

The pillow was slipped back under his head and Cody left the room, making his way back to the front door, and into the night.

When the doctor discovered Tinkler the following morning, he assumed that the lawyer had died in his sleep. The next body he saw, however, held no doubt about the way he'd died. A knife had been driven up between Cody's ribs from behind and into his heart.

Beth Morris was about to get more bad news – and her troubles were only just beginning.

Andrews placed the piece of paper on the desk for Brotherton to see. It was a little after eight, and the timber man had been waiting for Andrews to come to his office for a couple of hours. And he wasn't happy about it.

'Took your damned time,' he growled.

The killer shrugged. 'It's done. You got what you wanted.'

Brotherton took up the will and read it. 'It really does seem that Morris didn't trust his son with his ranch after all. Did you have any trouble?'

'Nope.'

'Right, as soon as the new sheriff gets here we'll move our equipment out there and start work. With the signed document allowing us access, there's nothing Beth Morris can do.'

'Are you still going to pay the money to her?' Andrews asked.

'Sure, though by the time I write in some deductions, there won't be much left at all,' Brotherton smiled cruelly. 'Go and find Vince for me. I have a job for him.'

'You want me to what?' Vince snapped.

'Should I say it slower? I want you to hold up the stage tomorrow and kill the man that Curtis and the whore have coming to town on it. His name is Myers, so the telegrapher said.'

'I don't mind killing for you,' Vince said. 'Especially when the money is right, but in the last couple of days we've killed a sheriff, that rancher, his son, the lawyer's been dealt with, and two of my men as well as one of yours. You go holding up a stage and killing a passenger on that and you're going to have marshals crawling up your ass to find out what the hell is going on.'

'Technically, Cody killed his father and the lawyer,' Brotherton pointed out. 'Besides, Swiftcreek is a lawless town. The new sheriff should be able to sort

86

things out when he arrives. Now, are you going to do it, or not? I tell you what, I'll pay you an extra hundred dollars for it.'

'All right, I'll do it.'

'Good.'

The stage was six miles from town the next morning when Vince and Warren, a man in Brotherton's employ, stopped it. They'd picked out a narrow stretch of trail which wound its way between large stands of trees, one of which they'd felled across the trail so the stage couldn't pass.

When it rounded the curve and saw the obstacle, the driver hauled back on the reins. He cursed his luck and stomped on the brake lever while trying hard to get the four-horse team to stop. He managed to do just that before they crashed into the fallen tree. Beside him, the guard held hard to the seat so that he wouldn't be thrown clear, and inside, the passengers tried to do the same.

The stage rocked as they all gathered themselves, and the driver growled, 'Christ, Hank, that was close.'

'Not wrong, Pete, we . . . oh, shit.'

The driver noticed his guard's jaw drop and looked in the direction he stared. There in the middle of the trail stood two figures: both had pale sacks over their heads and guns in their hands.

'Throw the messenger gun down and then you two follow it,' a voice growled.

Hank the guard hesitated, and the speaker said in a harsh voice, 'Don't think about it. Do as you're told

87

and you'll live through this.'

The weapon hit the hard ground and the men climbed down. The driver said, 'We ain't hauling nothing of value.'

'That depends on what we're looking for,' Vince said. They moved around to the side and called to the passengers, 'Everybody out.'

The door swung open and the stage rocked as two well dressed men climbed down. One had grey hair and a lined face, while the other had darker hair and was more solidly built. Plus, he had a six-gun strapped about his waist.

'You, drop the gun,' Vince ordered and waited while the passenger unbuckled the gun belt in silence.

Once it was on the ground, Vince ordered them to step forward a few paces. After they'd done as he'd ordered the outlaw asked, 'Which one of you is Myers?'

No one moved.

Again Vince asked, this time with a little less patience. 'Which one of you is Myers?'

Still no answer.

Vince pointed his gun at the driver and thumbed back the hammer. Pete blanched and threw up his hands. 'Wait!'

'I'm Myers!' exclaimed the older man.

The outlaw turned and faced the older man. He smiled beneath his hood and said, 'That wasn't hard now, was it?'

Then he squeezed the trigger.

The six-gun in his hand bucked and the slug hammered into the man's chest. Myers was thrown

backwards in an awkward stumble and fell to the
ground. But Vince needed to make sure, and shot the
prone figure once more.

'Let's shoot the rest of them now,' Warren snapped.

'No. We ain't here to do that.'

'Aww, shoot, why not?'

'Because I said,' Vince growled. 'Come on.'

Before they disappeared into the trees, Vince and
Warren took the surrendered weapons and threw
them away. Less chance of them trying something that
way. Then they were in their saddles and riding hard
for town.

CHAPTER 9

It seemed to Curtis that every time he went to town of late, there was always bad news to greet him. That day wasn't much better. And although he didn't know it yet, it was about to get worse.

He'd come to Swiftcreek with Lester and Mary-Alice to meet the stage. They'd also decided to stock up on supplies while they were there. Once inside, the three of them found out the news about Cody Morris and Tinkler.

'Someone knifed Cody?' Curtis asked.

'Sure did,' the store clerk said. 'Same day as someone shot Tinkler the lawyer.'

'Does his sister know?'

'Sure. She's in town trying to sort out the whole blamed mess.'

Curtis glanced at Mary-Alice who was busy using Lester to help her look at cloth to make a new dress. Then he asked, 'What mess?'

'It seems that before he died, young Cody sold all of the timber rights to Brotherton. But Beth tells him that they weren't Cody's to sell. She says that her father left them equal shares in the ranch in his will.'

Curtis nodded. 'That's what she told me.'

'Well, it seems that will has gone and disappeared. They've hunted through that office high and low but it ain't there. Mighty convenient if you ask me.'

Curtis sighed. 'Yeah, mighty.'

'He's told her that as soon as the new sheriff takes over he's going to shift his men and equipment out there and start to work.'

'How'd Beth take that?'

'She told him that if anyone set foot on her range, she'd shoot them herself.'

'What about a judge?'

'Circuit judge don't get here for another two weeks. Not that it would do any good. Brotherton's the one with the signed piece of paper.'

'What piece of paper?' Mary-Alice asked. Curtis hadn't noticed her approach.

He told her about what had happened.

'Oh, dear. How dreadful. To lose her father and brother all within a few days.'

From outside came the thunder of hooves and the sound of iron rims. Then Curtis heard a shout. 'We was held up! They killed one of the passengers.'

Blood turned to ice water in Curtis's veins, for he knew who the dead passenger would be. He grabbed the Yellow Boy from where it leaned against the counter and said to Mary-Alice, 'Stay here and finish your shopping.'

By the time he stepped out on to the boardwalk, the

dead man had already been removed from the coach and lain down beside it.

Curtis hurried across to the stage. He pushed through the crowd and stared down at the dead man. 'Who is he?'

'Myers,' answered the other passenger without looking up. 'You know him?'

Curtis cursed under his breath. 'Was expecting him. What happened?'

The passenger looked up and both men were suddenly in shock.

'A pair of gunmen stopped the stage and asked for him,' the driver Pete said, taking over. 'Then they shot him down cold. They knew he was coming in on it. Don't know what he did, but someone didn't like him doing it.'

'What's going on here?' Brotherton asked, pushing through the crowd.

Curtis broke his gaze away from the passenger and snapped at the timber man, 'You should know. You were behind it.'

Brotherton faked innocence. 'I don't know what you mean.'

'That dead feller was coming in to buy up tracts of timber on our land. Was even going to pay more than you were. Somehow you found out and had him killed.'

Brotherton's eyes narrowed. 'I'd be careful with what you say, Curtis. False accusations might get you into trouble.'

It was then that El Tigre bared his claws. He

stepped in close and said in a low voice, 'If you send it my way, then send it shooting, because I'll kill it dead. There's a war coming, Brotherton, and when it's over, we'll see who's left standing.'

Not waiting for a reply, Curtis turned away from Brotherton and walked off. If he hadn't, El Tigre might have killed him then and there.

As he was walking away, Beth Morris caught his eye. He crossed over the street to her and looked at her. 'I'm sorry about your brother.'

Her reply was something he wasn't expecting: 'I need your help.'

He frowned. 'OK, what with?'

'Brotherton has a paper with my brother's signature on it giving him the rights to all of our timber. My brother couldn't have signed it because both he and I were to get the ranch.'

'Yet Brotherton has it and your father's will has disappeared.'

'Yes. And I know he's behind it. Tinkler is dead, and without that will I can't prove a thing.'

'What do you want me to do?'

'Brotherton is moving his equipment into place tomorrow and it will be set up on the range he is logging,' Beth explained. 'But to do that he needs to cross my land. It's the only way he can get there. I heard my father speak about you, Jim. About what you've done. I need you to stand with my men to stop them crossing my land. They need someone like you to lead them.'

'Is that all?'

She shook her head. 'You offered to find the killer of my father. I need you to find his will instead. Without that will, I stand to lose everything.'

He thought about it. Helping her out would provide the opportunity to check out her hands. 'All right, I'll help.'

'There you are.'

Curtis turned and saw Mary-Alice and Lester coming towards them. Her face softened when she saw Beth and she hurried up to her and took her by the hand. 'I'm so sorry about your father and brother. Please, if there is anything I can do. . . .'

'Can I borrow your man?' Beth blurted out.

Mary-Alice's face turned red. 'No. I mean yes. Ahh, I mean he's not my man.'

Her reply served to confuse Beth somewhat.

Curtis said, 'What she means is that we're business partners, no more.'

'Oh. Sorry.'

Curtis glanced at Lester. 'You'll need to step up while I'm gone. Keep close to the homestead and an eye out for anything that's not right. And don't try to take on anything by yourself. Brotherton is dangerous.'

'I'll be fine,' Lester said.

'Oh, I almost forgot,' Mary-Alice said. 'Did the man come on the stage?'

'Good to meet you, Mr Reynolds,' Brotherton greeted the stranger from the stage. 'You come highly recommended. I trust that your journey wasn't too uncomfortable?'

Reynolds stared at the man behind the desk then glanced at Vince. 'Let's just say that it was interesting.'

Vince's face remained passive. He'd heard a lot about Reynolds in his travels. After the war, Reynolds had taken up a sheriff's badge for a year or so. Then someone had come along and asked him to clean up a town in Texas that the carpetbaggers were having trouble with. They paid well. Really well, so he'd taken the job. Before long he was riding through Texas cleaning up one town after another. Somewhere along the way the lines became blurred and it became more about the money and less about the law.

Now it didn't matter which side he was on, so long as he got his money and the person paying him was happy.

Reynolds continued, 'We agreed on a price.'

'Yes. Five hundred up front and then two hundred per week.'

'That's right. Now, what do you want me to do?'

Brotherton smiled. 'Enforce the law.'

'Your law?'

'Of course.'

'Uh huh.'

'Tomorrow I intend to move men and equipment on to land I just acquired for logging. I want you to ride with them and see that they are left alone.'

'Acquired legally?'

'I have a piece of paper with a signature on it.'

Reynolds noticed that he didn't say yes.

Brotherton went on. 'There have been a lot of deaths about here lately that will need investigating.

95

I'll give you the details about them later. If possible, I'd like it so that something was laid at the feet of a certain man we're having trouble with. Get rid of him and I'll double the five hundred.'

'Who?'

'Feller called Jim Curtis.'

It would be, Reynolds thought. 'You got anything in mind?'

'He killed three of my men.'

'Witnesses?'

'What do you want witnesses for?' Vince asked. 'I'd have thought that wouldn't matter to you.'

Reynolds let his cold stare settle on the man he was sure had held up the stage. 'It doesn't.'

'I can find as many as you need,' Brotherton said. 'I don't care if he's found not guilty at the trial. By then it won't matter.'

'And if he won't come quietly?'

Brotherton's eyes flared. 'Then kill him, damn it. Do I have to spell it out?'

'Nope, I reckon you don't.'

CHAPTER 10

There was only one trail to the timber country that Brotherton now claimed as his, and it cut right through Circle M. And as the wagons approached Circle M range loaded with men and equipment, Jack Reynolds noticed the strung-out line of riders along the crest of the ridge the wagons needed to take.

A quick count had them at eight, and the timber men had them outnumbered as well as outgunned. But maybe it could be resolved peacefully with no bloodshed. After all, there was the signed piece of paper in his pocket.

When he got close enough to make out faces clearly, his heart sank. There, sitting his horse at the centre of the line, was Jim Curtis. Right then he knew that there would be no peace. They drew up on the rutted trail when there was twenty feet between them. Out front was Reynolds, Vince and Andrews. On either side of Curtis was Beth and Sam, her new foreman.

Every one of the Circle M riders had rifles ready to

use. Except for Curtis. He had a messenger gun. Nothing deterred an ornery man like a double load of buckshot.

'Howdy, Jim,' Reynolds said.

'Captain.'

Confused glances shot between those on both sides.

'Been a while,' Curtis continued.

Reynolds nodded. 'It has. How you been keeping?'

'Fine, fine,' Curtis said as both men skirted the issue confronting them. 'I see you've got some new friends.'

'It is what it is. You've been busy since the war.'

'Could say the same about you.'

Finally, 'Shall we discuss what's about to happen here?'

'What's about to happen?'

Reynolds reached into his pocket and took out the piece of paper. He moved his horse closer to Curtis and passed him what he had.

Curtis read it and handed it back. 'The kid never had the power to sell it to Brotherton. What you've got there needs two signatures. The old man left the ranch to both his kids.'

'You have a copy of it?'

'It's disappeared,' said Beth. 'And the lawyer has been killed so we can't ask him. But there is one thing I can do. To get to where you want to go you have to cross Circle M range. But this is as far as you go. If you want to get there, find another way.'

'From what I've been told, there's no other way.'

'Hell, let's just shoot our way through,' Andrews

snarled. 'We got them outnumbered.'

Curtis moved the messenger gun so that it was pointed at the killer. 'Have at it. But you won't get two feet.'

'Whoa, Jim. We don't want a bloodbath, do we?'

'I guess that's up to Brotherton.'

Reynolds sighed. 'I didn't want to have to do this, Jim, but I've received a complaint about you killing three men. I guess now is as good a time as any to take you in.'

Curtis' face remained passive. He said, 'It was self-defence, Captain. They tried and lost.'

'I guess then we'll work it out in town.'

'I ain't going anywhere.'

'You don't really want to shoot it out with me, do you? We go way back, Jim. Come in and I'll sort it out.'

Reynolds was right. Curtis didn't want to kill his former commanding officer. 'All right. But there is one condition.'

'What is it?'

'No one tries to cross Circle M land until this all goes before a judge.'

'OK,' Reynolds said. 'I'll see what I can do.'

Curtis passed the messenger gun to Sam. 'Take this, I'll be back.'

'We ain't taking all of this equipment back to town,' Andrews growled.

The new sheriff shrugged. 'Leave it here then.'

'What if they try to damage it?'

'Then leave some people to keep an eye on it. Come on, Jim, let's get this sorted out.'

Beth said, 'Be careful, Jim. I don't like this.'

99

'I'll be fine, Beth. The captain will see me right.'

Reynolds smiled at her. 'He'll be fine, ma'am.'

The cell door clanged shut behind Curtis and almost immediately his blood ran cold. 'I don't see why you have to lock me up. There were plenty of witnesses.'

'Makes it official. It won't be for long. I'll go and make some enquiries and be right back.'

'Can you answer something for me, Captain?'

'What?'

'Are the stories true?'

'I could ask you the same thing, Jim.'

Curtis nodded. 'I guess you could.'

'They were tough times after the war.'

'Yeah. They were. A man did what he could to get by.'

'He did,' Reynolds agreed. 'I took up a badge and you went to Mexico to join the revolution. Made a name for yourself, from what I heard.'

'You too.'

'Good with a gun.'

'They say that about you.'

'Interesting, ain't it?' Reynolds commented. 'Both of us here in this town. Good at what we do. Another war going on. Yep, real interesting.'

Right then, when Curtis looked deep into Reynolds' eyes, he knew that before this was all over, one of them would be dead.

'Now is the time to move,' Brotherton said with confidence. 'With Curtis locked away, we can kill two birds with one stone.'

'I'm willing,' said Andrews, eager to spill more blood.

'Tell us what you want done,' Vince said.

Reynolds stood near the door while the discussion continued.

'We now have the chance to take the northern stand from that damned Mary-Alice and we can shift the equipment on to the Circle M,' Brotherton explained.

'I'll take the woman,' Andrews' voice was cold. 'I owe her.'

'I don't want her dead. Just take her somewhere and convince her to sign the land over to us. Burn her house and everything else as well. We won't be needing it.'

Andrews grunted. 'What do you want done with her when it's signed?'

'Kill her.'

'No!' Reynolds snapped. 'Let her go.'

The three men stared at him. Vince sneered at him. 'What's this? A killer with a conscience?'

'Let's just say I don't like killing women.'

'I don't care who I kill,' Andrews snapped.

Reynolds nodded. 'Figured as much. I'll put it another way. You do, and I'll kill you.'

Andrews squared up his shoulders and let his hand drop to his six-gun in a threatening gesture.

In a low voice, Reynolds said, 'Think about it.'

A long silence enveloped the room, an icy chill pervading the air, and just when it seemed that blood was about to be spilled, Brotherton's voice cut through the tension. 'All right, have it your way. Let her live. It won't much matter once we have it anyway.'

Happy with that, Reynolds asked, 'What do you want me to do with Curtis?'

'Investigate the shooting. It'll keep him out of the way while we do what we have to. Then let him go when we're done. Or kill him, it don't matter.'

'When do you want that equipment moved?' Vince asked.

'Tonight. Get it done.'

'And the woman?' said Andrews.

'No time like the present. Where are you going to take her?'

'There's an old cabin in the shadows of Crazy Woman Peak. I'll take a couple of men and head there with her.'

Brotherton's face grew hard. 'I don't need to tell you that there is a lot of money riding on the outcome of this. Don't let me down.'

'Well, am I getting out of here or what?' Curtis asked Reynolds.

The last rays of a reddish sunset shining through the barred back window of the jail told Curtis that he'd been there too long.

'Not today, Jim. I'm still looking into things. I have to tell you the people I talked to haven't convinced me that it was self-defence.'

Curtis couldn't believe what he was hearing. 'It might help if you didn't talk to just Brotherton's men.'

'I'll see what I can dig up tomorrow. Who knows, a new day might bring a few changes.'

There was something strange in the way Reynolds said it. 'What's that supposed to mean?'

'What?'

'The way you said that last bit.'

Reynolds shrugged. 'Nothing to it.'

Curtis knew he was lying. 'Why did you throw your lot in with Brotherton, Captain? He's bad through and through. The man I knew was different.'

'The war changes a man, Jim. You know that. You can't tell me it didn't change you.'

What he said was true.

'So that's how it's going to be?'

'Like I said, it'll all be different tomorrow.'

'Son of a bitch.'

'I've been called worse. Brotherton wants you dead, but I'd prefer not to have it that way. So, I just keep you locked away until it's over. But don't make the mistake that I won't do it. Old times only get you so far.'

CHAPTER 11

Mary-Alice woke to the sound of a horse's snort out in the yard. She lay there for a moment before hearing it again. A flicker of nervousness ran through her body.

'Lester, someone's outside.'

Beside her, the lump under the blankets stirred. 'Hmm?'

'Someone is out in the yard.'

'Are you sure?'

'Yes.'

Lester threw back the blankets and sat on the side of the bed. He strained to hear but no sound came. He waited a moment longer then rose to his feet and began to cross to the window. Before he reached it, the orange glow emanating from outside was obvious, and growing brighter.

'Good Lord, Mary, the bunkhouse is on fire.'

'Oh, no,' Mary-Alice gasped.

'There's three riders in the yard. They're going for the barn.'

Lester pulled his pants on and dashed for the front

door where a Henry leaned. He grasped it and burst through the doorway and out into the firelit yard. He levered a cartridge into the breech and snapped off a shot at the man with the flaming torch.

The slug flew wide and the rider threw the torch in through the open doors of the barn.

Lester jacked another round in and sighted along the barrel of the weapon. One of the other riders fired and he felt a deep burn in his side. The force of the blow from the bullet spun him halfway around.

Somewhere in the distance, Lester heard Mary-Alice cry out while he fought to bring the Henry back around. He had to protect Mary. He had assured Curtis that he would.

He felt weak but there was no give up in him. Lester managed to get the Henry back into line but never pulled the trigger. Instead, another bullet crashed into him, knocking him off his feet. This one buried deep in his chest.

Mary-Alice screamed and rushed to his side. She knelt in the dirt and cried over Lester's unconscious form.

'Get her up,' Andrews snarled. 'Then burn the house.'

'No!' Mary-Alice gasped.

One of the men grabbed a handful of hair and dragged her to her feet. She winced at the burning pain that seared her scalp. Mary-Alice bunched her fist and smashed it into the man's face. The assailant spat blood then returned the favour in spades.

Mary-Alice slumped to the ground, stunned. It

made her more manageable and he picked her up and carried her across to Andrews. 'Here, take the bitch.'

Andrews laid her face down in front of him. 'Hurry up and burn it so we can get the hell out of here.'

The man ran across to join his *compadre* and took a second torch from him. Then they set about igniting everything that would burn. Come morning, the only thing that should be left would be blackened ruins.

The dawn was cold. A pale pink light on the eastern horizon heralded its arrival and the five Circle M riders sat huddled around the small fire, trying to keep warm.

Sam sipped his pitch-black coffee, then blew on it before repeating his action. Beside him, a young cowboy asked, 'You reckon they might try again today?'

Sam shrugged. 'Who knows? You heard what the sheriff said.'

One of the other hands gave a cynical chuckle.

'What's up with you?'

The hand, whose name was Miller, said, 'Do you really believe that, Sam?'

'Why not?'

'Because it could be just a way of getting Curtis out of the picture. We all know that the sheriff was brought in by Brotherton.'

Sam nodded and sipped his coffee again.

'What's that?' another hand said.

All of them stopped what they were doing and listened intently. At first, it was hard to distinguish the sound from all the others brought about with the dawn. But after a few moments, the steady drumming grew louder.

'Riders coming!' Sam shouted and lunged for his Henry rifle. 'Quick, move.'

Topping the rise, the riders swept down upon the hands. Gunfire erupted immediately, and Miller fell, a horrible wound in his throat spraying blood.

Sam swung his Henry up and snapped off a shot. It flew wide and he jacked another round into the breech. But the surprise was complete.

Hands started to cry out as lead found flesh. Then Sam felt a hammer blow to his guts and all the air rushed from his lungs. He doubled over and slumped to his knees. In his desperation to suck some air back in, his mouth opened and closed futilely.

Then a second bullet struck him, this one high up in his chest. His mouth stopped moving and his eyes glazed over. Very slowly, the foreman of the Circle M ranch slumped sideways and fell onto the ground.

Vince hauled his horse to a halt and turned to shout back down the slope. 'Get them wagons moving!'

'One of them got away!' a gunman shouted.

'Don't worry about him now. We have to get this equipment moving. Get it done.'

Beth wasn't long out of bed when the wounded rider came into the ranch yard. He slopped about in the saddle and when the horse slid to a stop, he fell to the ground beside it. One of the hands called out and rushed over to the fallen man.

Beth hurried outside and saw a huddle of her hands gathered around the figure on the ground. 'What's going on?'

'It's Zeke,' a voice told her. 'He's been shot. It seems that Brotherton's men hit them this morning not long after first light.'

Beth looked down at Zeke and saw the bloody hole in his chest. It was ragged and she guessed that it was an exit wound, the result of him being shot in the back.

'They were meant to wait,' she said. 'The sheriff told us.'

'Brotherton's sheriff,' a hand named Teller pointed out.

Beth fixed her gaze on him. 'Ride and get the doctor. I'll follow and see the sheriff. A couple of you get out there and check on the others. However, do not go after Brotherton's men. Am I understood?'

'Yes, ma'am,' they answered.

'Someone saddle me a horse.'

The four riders climbed higher through the trees towards a grey-faced mountain with a snow-capped peak. Every part of Mary-Alice's body ached from the rock of the bay horse beneath her, mostly to do with the way she was tied to the saddle.

But that wasn't the only thing creating her ache. The memory of Lester being shot down before her had triggered a deep throb in her core, unlike anything that she'd felt since her husband had been killed.

'How much further have we got to go?' she asked Andrews.

'Until I say stop,' he snapped. 'Now shut up.'

The horses kept on for another hour before a log cabin came into view at the edge of a large stand of tall pines. They drew up outside and the men swung down. Andrews untied Mary-Alice while the other pair, Kent and Brooks, checked the cabin. Emerging through the doorway a short time later, they conferred briefly with Andrews before taking the horses around the back.

'Get inside,' the killer snapped at Mary-Alice.

'What do you want with me?'

'Your land.'

'No.'

'Then get inside. You'll be here a while.'

By mid-morning, Curtis was getting nervous. He knew that something was happening, but had no idea what, and his mind ran rife with countless possibilities. When Beth showed up, some of the pieces dropped into place.

She pushed in through the jailhouse door and glanced about until she saw Reynolds pouring himself a drink from atop a pot-bellied stove.

'You're a dirty liar,' she snarled at him. 'You lied and now my men are dead!'

The lawman placed the pot back on the stove before turning toward her, and said, 'I don't know what you mean.'

'Horseshit. You know exactly what I mean.'

'What happened, Beth?' Curtis asked from within his cell.

'The bastards jumped my men this morning. Only one of them got away. They're probably at the trees by now.'

Curtis stared at Reynolds. 'Was this part of it? Lock me up so I wouldn't be a problem. You told me they would wait.'

Reynolds shrugged.

A slow-building anger began to roil Curtis' guts. 'What about our place? Was it a target too?'

Again, a shrug.

'You son of a bitch,' he cursed at Reynolds. 'Let me out of here.'

'Can't do that, Jim. Haven't finished my investigation.'

Curtis grasped the bars of the cell, his knuckles whitening. Only it wasn't Curtis, it was El Tigre. 'Let me the hell out!'

'Calm down, Jim. I should be done in a day or two. I can't find all of the witnesses.'

'You son of a bitch. You ain't even trying.'

Reynolds just stared at him.

'Beth, can you get someone from town to go out and check on Mary-Alice and Lester? Someone you trust?'

Beth nodded. 'I'll do it right away.'

'You'd be best to stay out of this, ma'am,' Reynolds said gently.

She gave him a cold stare and snapped, 'You go to

110

hell!' Then she whirled and hurried out the door.

'I thought more of you than this, Captain,' Curtis said.

'Like I said, things change.'

'I'll tell you this, Reynolds,' El Tigre seethed. 'If anything has happened to them, I'll kill every man responsible. Including your boss.'

'Let it go, Jim. It's too much for one man.'

'I knew a Mexican who told me that once. His name was Ramirez. He was an officer in Maximilian's army. They buried him two days later. Once I start, I don't stop, Reynolds.'

The sheriff noted that Curtis had stopped using the word captain, and along with its disappearance, he figured that any trace of respect was gone too.

'I don't want to have to kill you, Jim,' Reynolds said.

El Tigre stepped up to the bars and hissed, 'I doubt you'd be able to.'

CHAPTER 12

Ace Hennessy, the livery owner of Swiftcreek, topped a low rise and cursed at the sight before him. The blackened ruins of buildings stood out like dark beacons against the green backdrop of the grass and trees behind the yard, faint wisps of smoke still rising from each burned pyre.

He urged his horse forward and it walked down the slope. On entering the yard, his eyes alighted upon the still form of Lester. Hennessy climbed down and checked for signs of life. The man had been shot in the side and chest. Both wounds had long stopped bleeding.

Hennessy bent low.

'Son-of-a-bitch,' he muttered. 'Lester, can you hear me?'

His inquiry was met with silence.

Hennessy gave him a gentle shake. 'Lester? You hear me?'

A moan escaped his lips.

The livery owner glanced around. 'Lester, where's

Mary-Alice?'

'They took her,' he mumbled. 'I came to . . . when . . . they rode . . . out.'

'Who was it?'

'Don't . . . know.'

'Hang in there, Lester. I'll get the wagon hooked up and get you back.'

'Tell . . . Curtis.'

'Don't worry, Lester. He'll be told.'

'You lumberjacks get out there and start felling trees while the rest of us get this equipment set up,' foreman Dave Tyler ordered the six burly men before him. 'Take your sidearms as well.'

A solidly built man named Bower who led the lumberjack team asked, 'You think they'll come after us?'

Tyler glanced at Vince. The gunman said, 'Never can be too careful.'

The axemen wandered up the slope until they reached the trees and started in on bringing them down. Around a hundred yards back in the gloom, a dark shadow slunk away behind a large rock. It was followed by four more.

Then a lonesome howl echoed through the forest. The lumberjacks stopped and stared at each other. Bower said, 'Ain't heard one of them around here in a long while.'

'Let's hope it stays away,' another man said.

Bower grunted. 'Come on, let's get some of these trees down so they can be milled.'

*

113

'You changed your mind yet?' Andrews asked Mary-Alice.

She stuck out her chin, her eyes full of defiance. 'About what?'

'You know.'

With a shake of her head, she said, 'Not likely.'

'You know, things can get a lot worse for you.'

'You mean worse than being held here with scum like you?'

His open hand flashed out and the palm caught Mary-Alice across her right cheek. The blow wasn't hard enough to draw blood, but it stung and turned her cheek a scarlet colour.

'That's just a taste,' Andrews hissed.

Mary-Alice's eyes sparkled. 'Would you like me to turn my back so you can shoot me?'

This time the vicious strike rocked her, drawing blood. Andrews said, 'I'd advise you to think carefully about what you say next.'

But the change in Mary-Alice was complete as she had reverted to the woman she'd once been. The death of her husband and everything that had ensued since then had seen to that. She spat blood and growled in a low voice, 'I'm going to cut your damned heart out.'

Her words should have shocked her. They were something that she would expect Curtis to say. But she was now devoid of emotion, except for the burning hatred that she felt for the man before her.

Instead of striking her again, Andrews gave her a mirthless smile. 'Get in line.'

114

'I'll be the one in front.'

He stared at her and shook his head. It was going to be a long stay.

Beth Morris entered the sparse and dusty jail and walked straight past Reynolds and up to the cell where Curtis was being held. From the expression on her face, he knew instantly that the news was bad.

'The man I sent out to check just brought Lester in. He's been shot, and the doctor isn't sure if he'll make it.'

'What about Mary-Alice?'

'Whoever it was, took her.'

'Christ,' Curtis seethed. He looked past her to Reynolds. 'This is your damned fault.'

'That's not all,' Beth said. 'They burned it. All of it. There's nothing left.'

'Let me out of here, Reynolds!'

The sheriff did something that Curtis never expected. He smiled. Then he shook his head. 'I'll let you out when the time is right.'

El Tigre stared long and hard at Beth. She nodded almost imperceptively as the unspoken words passed between them. After which she turned and left. Then he redirected his malevolent stare to Reynolds. 'There's a storm coming. If I was you, I wouldn't be here when it breaks.'

'Is that some kind of threat, Jim?'

Curtis shook his head. 'Nope. Straight up fact.'

Reynolds left the jail and made his way along to

Brotherton's office. His transit was followed by a myriad of stares, but none more closely than that of Beth Morris. As soon as she saw him disappear through the door she hurried back to the jail.

She entered the office and crossed to the cell. 'I have to hurry before he comes back.'

'I wasn't sure if you'd got it right.'

'The stare?'

'Yes.'

'Do you know where the keys are?'

'I think they're in the top drawer of the desk.'

Beth checked and found them there. She unlocked the cell door and let Curtis out. 'What are you going to do now?'

'I have to find Mary-Alice and the will that your father left. Without that, Brotherton will still be able to keep possession of the timber on your range.'

'Why not just kill him and be done with it?'

Curtis found his Remington and the Yellow Boy. He gave her a grim smile. 'It'll more than likely come to that. But I want that bastard to squirm first. Besides, if I go after him now, he's got me a touch outgunned. Might pay to whittle them down first. Stay close to home, Beth. This is going to get more than a little out of hand.'

She watched him strap on the gun belt. 'But I want to help.'

'You've done enough. Safer this way. Bring all your hands in and wait for word from me. Brotherton may not stop at just the timber. He may want more.'

'OK.'

'Right, let's go,' Curtis said. 'Out the back.'

They slipped out the rear door and once outside, he said, 'Go home. I'll be fine now.'

Beth reached out and touched his arm. 'Good luck. Be safe.'

Curtis reached the livery and found Hennessy in the loft, forking down fresh hay. The livery man seemed surprised to see him.

'I need a horse,' Curtis told him.

'How'd you get out?' Hennessy asked.

'Had a little help,' Curtis explained. 'Horse?'

'Sure. Are you going after your woman?'

'She ain't my woman.'

'There ain't much left out there,' Hennessy told him as he walked along to a stall near the rear of the stables.

Curtis frowned. 'You've been out there?'

'Sure. Beth Morris had me go check.'

'Did you talk to Lester?'

Hennessy took a bay gelding out of the stall and began to saddle it. 'He weren't really up to talking when I found him. Just told me more or less what happened and that the woman was took.'

'Didn't say who it was?'

'Nope.'

It was then that Curtis noticed the brand on the horse's rump. It was a Circle M. 'You giving me a Circle M horse?'

Hennessy shrugged. 'The owner won't be needing it.'

117

'The owner?'

'Cody Morris.'

Curtis' next action gave the livery man reason to pause. He went around the animal and started to check its shoes. The third one was the one he sought. It had the nick in it. 'Son of a bitch.'

He now knew who'd killed Morris. But how in hell was he going to tell Beth?

'What was that?' asked Hennessy.

'I said thanks for the horse.'

'Be careful out there,' he warned Curtis. 'I got me a feeling that something ain't right.'

'I've had that same feeling ever since I got here,' Curtis murmured. 'Tell me, are Vince and Andrews in town?'

'Vince is. Ain't seen Andrews.'

'Thanks.'

'You think Andrews is the man you're looking for?'

Curtis swung up on to the horse. 'I'd be surprised if it wasn't.'

He rode out of the livery stable via the back door in order to remain unseen. But he was seen.

Hennessy had just returned to his chores when Vince appeared. He stared up at the livery man and gave him a cruel smile. Horror at the realization of what it meant, suddenly etched itself on the face of the man in the loft. Vince said, 'It's time me and you had a talk.'

CHAPTER 13

'He's gone,' Reynolds said with an air of calmness.

'What?' Brotherton snapped.

'I said, he's gone.'

'Who?'

'Curtis, of course.'

'How the hell did he get out?' Brotherton snarled.

'I don't know.'

'I told you to kill him.'

'I might have to yet.'

Brotherton shook his head. 'No, you will. Enough is enough. I want him shot on sight. Got it?'

Reynolds remained silent.

'Got it?' Brotherton asked again with more emphasis.

'Yeah. Got it. Don't push me.'

'While I'm paying you, Reynolds, I'll push as hard as I damned well please.'

Reynolds turned away and began to walk out.

'Where in hell are you going?' Brotherton snapped.

Reynolds didn't bother to look back. 'To find Curtis.'

*

Curtis surveyed the scene before him and cursed softly under his breath. Everywhere he looked there were blackened piles of charred timber. Every shred of their hard work had been destroyed in what would seem to be a blink of an eye. Well, someone would pay.

He scouted the yard for sign and found a lot of it. The most disturbing was the darkened patch where Lester had lain bleeding.

There were three riders and they'd headed west towards the mountains. Obviously one of them was riding double. He stared in the direction that the riders had taken and saw the grey-faced peak surrounded by endless tracts of pine. He turned and walked back towards the horse which stood ground-hitched in the centre of the yard.

Curtis was about to swing into the saddle when the snap and hiss of a bullet passed close to his head followed by the whiplash of a rifle. He reeled away from the horse, taking the Yellow Boy from the saddle scabbard.

Hands worked fast as Curtis levered a round into the breech of the Winchester. He ran across to the water trough as several bullets chased him. Small geysers of dirt kicked up around Curtis' feet. He dived behind the trough just as a slug buried deep into its thick timber side.

While the echoes of the shots rolled away across the landscape, a voice called out. 'It's just you and me, *amigo!*'

Vince!

'The time has come for the end of El Tigre!'

'You think you're good enough, Vince?'

'Sure do.'

'You've made a piss poor effort of it so far. You had a clean shot and you missed. What happened? The shakes get to you?'

Another shot rang out. This one more from frustration than anything else. Curtis still couldn't work out how the hired gun had managed to get so close. He figured that Vince must have seen him ride out of town. Another bullet smashed into the side of the trough.

Curtis eased around the end of his scant wooden cover, trying to get a line on Vince's position. Another gunshot told Curtis that he was just outside the yard behind a clump of rocks. Beyond that was the tree line, and he figured that the killer had used them to gain proximity without being noticed.

The Yellow Boy came forward and Curtis fired a shot off at the rocks. He saw the puff of stone chips from the bullet strike. Then he waited, but not for long. Vince's black hat appeared slowly above the rock and Curtis sent another .44 Henry slug in his direction.

The hat seemed to flip in the air and disappeared. The top of Vince's head was now exposed, but by the time Curtis was ready to fire another shot it was gone.

'Damn!' Curtis shouted. 'Almost had you then, Vince. Maybe should have lowered my aim half an inch.'

When no answer came, he turned his head and tried to find a way out of his predicament. They could both remain behind cover until the cows came home, but nothing would be accomplished by that, except stalling Curtis from getting on with his hunt.

Directly behind him was the rubble of the barn. He seemed to be out of other options. Curtis got down on his belly and crawled towards the blackened debris. When he reached it he realized that to go around it, he would be exposed to Vince's position.

He drew in a breath and started forward, straight into the ash and burnt remains. The fine black ash dust clung to everything it touched, and he was soon coated in a layer of the stuff from head to foot. It got up his nose, in his mouth and eyes. Some sections forced him to rise marginally to make his way over them and under others. But once he was safely through, he was totally unrecognizable.

On the other side, he paused to wipe away most of the ash and grit from the rifle. He only hoped that it would still fire.

Rising into a crouch, he was about to move when a shot came and a piece of charred wood beside him exploded in a spray of black splinters.

'Damn it!' Curtis cursed. More shots. He was pinned down. 'Well done, idiot.'

He looked up at the sun. Perhaps three more hours of daylight left. It was going to be a long wait.

'Who's got the woman, Vince?'

'Why do you think I'd tell you, Curtis?'

'I just thought that since you're so convinced you're

going to kill me, you might as well tell me.'

A laugh reached his ears. 'Maybe I'll let you die wondering.'

'So, where did you take her?'

'I didn't take her anywhere. Maybe she's under all that mess of the house.'

'Did Andrews take her to Brotherton?'

'No.'

Curtis smiled. 'So, Andrews did take her?'

There was a pause and Curtis thought that Vince's silence was him admonishing himself for his mistake. 'I didn't say that.'

'Nope, you didn't.'

Silence descended and no more was said. Curtis lay there thinking about Mary-Alice and Lester. Also, of Beth Morris and what had driven Reynolds to become the man he was.

Then a sound reached his ears. Hoofbeats. Curtis frowned. Coming or going?

Going.

With caution, he rose to his knees and peered over the pile of rubble in front of him.

Nothing happened.

Curtis climbed to his feet, the Yellow Boy ready in his grasp. He braced himself for the whiplash of Vince's gun but everthing remained silent.

'Run away, did you?' Curtis murmured. 'Well, you'll keep. First I've got to get the woman back.'

Following the trail until he could see no more, he then made a small fire to camp by. He would continue the following morning. With any luck, Mary-Alice would still be alive when he found them. After all, if they wanted her dead, they would have killed her at the house. Which meant they wanted something from her. Hopefully, he would find her before that happened.

Beside the campfire that night, the nightmare came back. He'd not had it for a long time. Thought it gone. Obviously, it hadn't.

El Tigre's hand clamped down over Nita's mouth and he whispered harshly in her ear. 'Keep quiet. There are soldiers outside!'

Her eyes widened in the moonlight which flooded through the adobe building. His hand released, and she whispered, 'How did they find you were here in Zamora?'

El Tigre shook his head. 'I don't know.'

Nita's voice grew cold. 'You were betrayed.'

'Most probably.'

'Where is Emilio?' she asked, thinking of their son.

'He is still asleep in his crib,' El Tigre assured her. 'I have to go out there.'

Nita grasped his arm. 'No. You can't. They will kill you.'

'And they will kill you and Emilio if I don't.'

He rose from the bed and started to cross towards the door of the one-roomed adobe house they shared.

'Wait!' Nita snapped. 'I am your wife.'

'It has to be, Nita. For you and Emilio.'

The door swung open and El Tigre stepped through and out into the moonlit yard. 'I believe you are looking for me?'

A voice said, '*Sí.*'

'Well, here I am.'

'You are El Tigre?'

'I am.'

'Where is your woman?'

'She has nothing to do with this.'

'I will be the judge of that,' the man said.

'I am here,' Nita said and stepped up beside her husband.

El Tigre's anger flared. 'Go back inside, damn it.'

'I belong with you.'

'You belong with our son. Go!'

She made to turn away when the officer in charge stopped her. 'Wait!'

El Tigre stepped in front of her. 'She has nothing to do with this. Let her be.'

'She is your wife. She has everything to do with this.'

'I said let her be, damn you!'

Suddenly Emilio's high-pitched cries sounded from inside. Nita said, 'I must go to my child.'

The officer's voice was emotionless. 'No, we will take care of him.'

Nita's blood ran cold as she realized what they intended to do. Her husband's voice cut through the air. 'Nita! Run! Get Emilio.'

El Tigre charged the horses to give his wife the precious time she needed to get inside to their son. But when the guns began to bark, she only made it as far as the door before she was cut down by four bullets.

'No!' El Tigre screamed. 'No!'

'No! Nita!' Curtis cried out, and sat up abruptly in his blankets.

Sweat was beaded on his brow and his heart raced with the sudden anxiety of the nightmare. The soldiers had killed his wife and son. They'd shot him down where he stood. But they'd forgotten to check that El Tigre was dead.

The people of Zamora had found him to be alive and nursed him back to health. And after he'd put flowers on the grave of his wife and infant son, the Tiger had bared his teeth in spectacular fashion.

Curtis had gathered men around him from both sides of the border. Some from the war who'd fought for money, and peons who'd fought for their freedom. When he had amassed enough, he set them against the garrison where the man responsible for the deaths of his wife and child accommodated himself. By the time it was over, the garrison had been wiped out.

He'd never allowed himself to love a woman since.

Curtis fingered the puckered scars beneath his shirt. There were three of them. By some miracle, none of the bullets had struck anything vital.

He still blamed himself for Nita and Emilio's deaths.

Somewhere in the distance, Curtis heard a wolf howl. He laid back down and closed his eyes. Sleep was a long time coming.

Curtis was up just before the sun the following

morning, and in the saddle shortly thereafter. He picked up the trail straightaway and followed its unde-viating path towards the mountain.

The narrow path wound its way through the timber, climbing steadily, then dropping every now and then. It crossed a couple of mountain streams and through a large green meadow lit by bright sunlight. Eventually, about mid-morning, a cabin appeared, and Curtis knew with certainty that this was where he would find them.

He dismounted, stayed in the trees, and circled the cabin until he was behind it. There he could see the three horses in a makeshift corral. Curtis checked to see that there was a round under the hammer of the Yellow Boy. He was about to approach the cabin when a man appeared.

Brooks hurried around the corral and turned so his back was facing Curtis. Then he dropped his pants, revealing the stark white skin of his rump. He squatted down to do his business, which gave Curtis time to move in.

Brooks was still squatting when Curtis hit him with the stock of the Yellow Boy. With a grunt the man fell forward. 'Hate to be you when you wake up. At least you'll still be alive.'

He kept moving along the side of the rough-hewn cabin, stepping over weeds and rocks, and paused outside the window. From inside he heard a voice say, 'Have you changed your mind yet?'

'No,' Mary-Alice answered.

'I guess I'm going about this the wrong way, then,'

the man said, and Curtis heard the crack as Mary-Alice's face was slapped, followed by a choked gasp. Two more cracks came in quick succession.

Curtis gripped the Yellow Boy hard and his knuckles whitened. He ducked beneath the window and slipped around to the front of the cabin. He thumbed back the hammer of the Winchester and kicked the door with his boot, hard!

The door flew back on its hinges with a crash. Curtis stormed through the opening and brought up his gun on the first of the two startled men. The Yellow Boy roared impossibly loud in the confines of the small cabin, and Kent was hit hard in the chest with the .44 Henry slug. He was flung backwards, but tried desperately to keep his feet, before his legs gave out underneath him.

Kent collapsed, and Curtis worked the lever on the Yellow Boy and switched his aim. Still in shock, Andrews hadn't even reacted. He realized it was too late and raised his hands.

'I guess you got me,' he said, his tone laconic.

With a nod of his head, Curtis said, 'I guess I have.' Then he squeezed the trigger.

Mary-Alice jumped at the report of the Yellow Boy, then watched in horror when Andrews lurched back and fell across the chair behind him.

It collapsed with a clatter under his weight, and he ended up sprawled across the splintered mess. He didn't move.

'Are you OK, Mary-Alice?' Curtis asked her.

She came off the chair she was seated on and threw

herself at him. She buried her face into his chest and started to cry. 'Oh, Jim. Thank you. They were ghastly. They killed Lester. Shot him down cold.'

'No, Mary-Alice. Lester is still alive. He's at the doc's.'

She took a step back and looked up at him through tear-filled eyes. 'He's alive? Lester's alive?'

'Yes.'

'But it can't be. I saw him with my own eyes.' Her hand fluttered to her chest.

'He was the last I heard.'

Mary-Alice frowned at him. 'What are you doing here? Did the sheriff let you out?'

'Not exactly. Come on, we've got to get out of here.'

'Where are we going? They burned everything we built.'

'Yeah, I know. I'm going to take you to Beth Morris's. You can stay there while this all sorts itself out.'

'OK.'

They started towards the door and just before they walked outside, the still-stunned form of Brooks filled the doorway.

'What the hell?' he asked, bewildered.

Curtis' reflexes were like lightning and he brought the Yellow Boy swinging up so that the butt plate caught the man under his chin. He dropped like a stone, once again out like a flame in a rain storm. Then they disappeared outside.

CHAPTER 14

'I can't believe it,' Beth Morris said, aghast. 'Why? Why would he kill our father?'

Curtis and Mary-Alice had arrived back at the Circle M in the late afternoon and he had just now told her of his theory about her brother, Cody.

Curtis shrugged. 'I guess only he could have answered that. Not now though. Anyhow, the sign doesn't lie. He hid his horse and crept up and shot your father.'

Beth Morris shook her head. 'It would explain why he was in a hurry to sell the timber rights. But I'd like to know what happened to the money.'

'It's probably with your father's will. I'm going to see if I can find it tonight.'

'Where?' Mary-Alice asked.

'The most obvious place. Brotherton's office.'

'No!' both women gasped out at once.

'They'll kill you if they find you,' Beth pointed out.

'You can't do it,' said Mary-Alice. 'I couldn't stand it if you were killed because of me.'

'Just hold up,' Curtis urged them. 'First off, I ain't going to get killed. Second, even if they do find me, they'll have themselves a tiger by the tail.'

He gave them a wry smile but neither seemed to be impressed by his attempt at humour.

'That's not funny,' Mary-Alice scolded him.

Curtis nodded. 'Maybe not, but if I don't find that will, then Brotherton can do what he wants with all of that timber, and there is no way to stop him.'

'What will you do if you find it?' Beth asked.

'Bring it back here. If he does have it, it'll mean that he either killed Tinkler and took it, or . . .' he paused.

'What?' asked Mary-Alice.

'I think I know,' Beth said.

He gave her a reluctant stare.

Beth continued. 'It could mean that Cody killed Tinkler to get the will so he could sell the timber without any interference. And if he did, then Brotherton killed him for it.'

Curtis nodded. 'I'm sorry.'

Beth sighed. 'After what you've told me, I'm not surprised that it has led to this. Just be careful. I'm like Mary-Alice. I don't want you killed on my behalf.'

'I'll be fine.'

'I'll have one of the hands saddle your roan.'

He was surprised. 'It's here?'

Beth smiled. 'Like I said, I'll have it saddled.'

'Christ almighty! What in hell does it take to get a man killed around here?' Brotherton roared at Brooks who was nursing his aching head. 'Instead the bastard kills two more of my men and gets away with the Condon woman. First it was Reynolds let him escape, Vince tracked him to the ranch and let him go, and now this. I'm surrounded by idiots!'

Reynolds watched from his usual corner in Brotherton's office. He remained silent. Long ago he'd learned that anger wasn't a luxury he could afford. Anger caused mistakes to happen. Anger got you killed.

Vince said, 'I'd say Curtis and the woman have gone to the Circle M to hole up.'

Brotherton's eyes narrowed. 'Well, we sure as shit can't go riding on to that spread, can we? Not if we don't want to come up against all of their guns. Any suggestions?'

'We wait.'

All eyes were directed at Reynolds.

'Why should we do that?' Brotherton sneered.

'Because the man I know won't sit idle for long. He'll want to bring the fight to us.'

'So, we wait?'

'Uh huh.'

Brotherton shook his head. Other than risk losing more men, he had little choice. 'OK then. We wait. But you better be right.'

'He'll come.'

'Fine,' the timber man snapped. 'I need a drink. If you want me, I'll be at the Silver Aspen.'

Curtis hit the outskirts of Swiftcreek a little after ten that evening. He found a place to hide the roan and walked in on foot, keeping to the shadows.

His first point of call was the doctor to find out how Lester was doing.

'You're taking a chance coming here,' snapped grey-haired Doctor William Lewis when he opened his door to Curtis. 'Especially after you killed Ace Hennessy.'

Curtis pushed his way in through the open door. 'What the hell are you talking about?'

'You killing Hennessy, the livery owner.'

'He's dead?'

Lewis frowned. 'Yes, you killed him.'

'The hell I did,' Curtis growled. 'He was alive when I left. He helped me out by giving me a horse.'

'That's not the story that's going around.'

'Well, maybe you should find out who's telling the damned story,' Curtis snapped. 'Because I sure as hell didn't kill him.'

His remarks gave Lewis pause for thought. Then he said, 'All right, maybe you didn't, but how can you prove it?'

'I can't. How's Lester doing?'

'He's much better. I think he might actually make it.'

'That's something, anyway.'

'What are you doing in town?'

'I've come to pay Brotherton a visit.'

'Are you crazy?' Lewis blurted out.

'I need to find Morris's will.'

'You think Brotherton has it?'

'I guess I'll find out when I get over to his office.'

133

Lewis had an idea. 'Wait here. I'll go and see if he's there or not.'

'No, Doc, you stay out of this. I'll be fine. They'll kill you if they figure out that you were involved. Just get Lester better.'

'Good luck, Jim. Make that bastard pay for what he's done.'

'Thanks, Doc. I intend to.'

The office was empty when Curtis arrived. He peered in through a window, but all was in darkness. He tried it and he found it unlocked. Lifting the window sash high enough to climb through, he made it through the narrow space, closing it behind him.

Curtis found a lantern and lit it, having made sure all the curtains were closed before he did. Then he looked over the top of Brotherton's desk. He doubted it would be there in plain sight, but you never knew.

Next he tried the desk drawers. He found some papers there along with a small calibre six-gun, but not what he wanted.

'Damn it,' Curtis swore.

His gaze swept the room and stopped on the cabinet with three sets of drawers. He opened the top one and began going through it.

Curtis found what he wanted in the second drawer, folded and tucked away at the back. He carried it closer to the lamp and perused it quickly.

'That's interesting,' he murmured.

Curtis tucked it away in his pocket and looked around the office. His lips pressed together and scooped up the lantern from the desktop. 'What was it the bible said? Do unto others as they would to you? Something like that.'

Then with a sweep of his arm, he flung the lantern across the room. By the time he turned and walked out, the flames were already taking hold.

'FIRE!'

The shout echoed through the Silver Aspen Saloon and everyone stopped what they were doing to stare at the man in the doorway.

'Fire! The Brotherton office is on fire!'

There was a scramble towards the door as the crowd moved like a wave on the sand. Brotherton came out of his seat and almost knocked the table over. He started to push his way through the crush.

'Get out of the way, damn it!' he bellowed. 'Get out of the way!'

Reynolds came casually to his feet and walked up to the bar, his bootheels clunking loudly on the floorboards of the almost empty room. He grabbed a bottle of whiskey and poured some of the contents into a glass. Vince was the only other man left, and he stood further along the counter. He said, 'It was Curtis, wasn't it?'

The sheriff knocked back the whiskey and nodded. 'I'd say so.'

'You figure he's gone?'

Reynolds looked up to stare at the killer. His gaze drifted past the man's shoulder. 'Nope.'

Vince turned around and his jaw dropped.

Standing there with the Yellow Boy pointing toward them was Curtis. But there seemed to be something different about him. He had changed.

'Which one of you killed Hennessy?' Curtis inquired with a growl.

'You start the fire, Jim?' Reynolds asked.

'Yeah. Figured he deserved at least that.'

The sheriff nodded. 'Now you're here for what? Exact revenge?'

'Something like that.'

'Word is, it was you who killed the hostler.'

'You know that ain't true,' Curtis said, shifting his gaze towards Vince. 'How'd you find me, Vince?'

'Followed you.'

'You're a liar. Try again.'

'Saw you coming out of the livery.'

'Yeah. And then you killed Hennessy after you found out what you wanted to know.'

Vince nodded. 'Sure.'

Reynolds said, 'You have your answer, Jim. Now what?'

'You want in on this?'

'Nope, your fight.'

Curtis said to Vince, 'Go for your gun.'

The killer snorted. 'What? When you already have a gun on me? Nope. I don't think so. No chance for me in that.'

Lips peeled back from teeth as El Tigre smiled. 'It's all the chance you're going to get.'

'No chance at all.'

'Take it or leave it.'

'Go to hell!' Vince snarled.

'You first.'

Vince's hand went for his gun but as he'd stated, he had no chance. The Yellow Boy whiplashed, and the .44 Henry slug tore into his chest. It drove him back a few steps and he managed to use the edge of the bar to gather himself.

Curtis levered and fired twice more, each bullet slamming into flesh not far from the previous one. Red seemed to bloom on Vince's shirt front with each strike. Then the strength finally left his legs and he fell into a dead heap on the timber floor.

The Yellow Boy shifted its aim and settled on Reynolds' chest. The sheriff had not moved. He said, 'Are you going to use that?'

'Not yet.'

'Mind pointing it somewhere else?'

'Yeah. I do,' Curtis said. Then, 'Tell Brotherton this ain't over.'

'I'll do that.'

'One other thing.'

'What?'

'Leave. Just ride out, Captain, before it's too late.'

'I thought it already was.'

Curtis nodded. 'All right then, be seeing you.'

'Likewise.'

He backed out the way he'd come in through the back door and disappeared into the night while the rest of the town fought the blaze under the direction of an irate Brotherton.

*

The empty whiskey glass thumped down on the bar top with a loud clunk. Brotherton wiped at his face, smudging the soot even further. 'Gone! All of it. Christ! Burned to the ground. All because you didn't shoot your goddamned friend!'

Reynolds was silent.

'Well! Say something!'

'He's not my friend.'

'Well, shoot the son of a bitch then!' Brotherton seethed. He pointed at Vince's body that was still on the floor. 'Preferably before he kills all of my men.'

'He'll be back.'

'He said so, did he?'

Reynolds nodded.

'When he does, you kill him. It's what I'm damned well paying you for. Do it or I'll find someone who will.'

CHAPTER 15

Beth Morris' hand trembled while she read her father's will. An expression of disbelief was etched on her face. She shook her head. 'Why would he do this?'

Curtis took a sip of the coffee before him and said, 'He obviously didn't trust Cody.'

'But this gives me complete control over the whole of Circle M.'

'It does.'

'That's great,' Mary-Alice joined in. They were both still up when Curtis had arrived back at the ranch.

'But what do I do next?' Beth asked.

'Take your timber back,' Mary-Alice said, stating the obvious.

There was apprehension on Beth's face. 'How? He's not going to give it up without a fight. There is no lawyer in town since Tinkler was killed, and the sheriff works for Brotherton. As for the judge, who knows when he'll be here? And by then they could have a whole lot of forest down.'

'But surely there must be something you can do?'

139

Mary-Alice asked.

'There is,' Curtis said. 'But not at this time of night. Let's turn in.'

'But I want to hear your idea,' Beth argued.

Curtis drank the last of his coffee and rose to his feet. 'In the morning. Goodnight.'

Beth had a perplexed look on her face as she followed him. However, the one on Mary-Alice's was different. Hers was one of concern.

'Where are you going?' Mary-Alice asked Curtis early the next morning. He was thumbing fresh loads into the Yellow Boy while sitting in the sun, drinking his early morning coffee on the veranda.

'Going to move Brotherton's men on.'

'By yourself?'

Curtis nodded. 'Yeah.'

She gave him an incredulous look. 'You can't do that.'

'Someone has to. I don't see the sheriff doing it.'

'But, Jim, there'll be so many of them,' Mary-Alice pointed out.

'I'd best shoot them first then. What do you think?'

'This isn't funny,' she growled.

'I didn't say that it was.'

'What's going on?' Beth asked as she came out through the door.

'Jim is going to fight Brotherton's men on his own,' Mary-Alice informed her.

'What?'

'Uh huh. I told him it was a crazy idea.'

140

Curtis said, 'No you didn't.'

'Well, it is.'

Beth looked worried. 'I agree. It is crazy. At least take some of the hands.'

'No. They're only cattlemen, not killers. Which for this, they'll need to be. I'm better off on my own. Who knows, maybe Brotherton's men will just leave of their own accord.'

'Get the hell away from here before I bust you open with this axe,' Dave Tyler snarled. 'Go on, get.'

'I was hoping we could do this the friendly way,' Curtis said. 'I guess I was wrong.'

'Damn straight you were wrong,' Bower hissed from behind him. 'Get back on your horse, killer.'

When Curtis had arrived at the lumber camp, most of the men there were busy working. It didn't last, however. Once they saw the rider they all stopped and moved in on him.

Curtis had dismounted and unsheathed the Yellow Boy. He thumbed back the hammer and waited for the welcoming committee.

They'd moved around him in almost a full circle, armed with axes, branches and even spare handles.

Curtis turned to look at each man, coming back to face Dave Tyler. 'It doesn't have to be this way. Beth Morris has legal right to this land. It was never her brother's to sell. Which means you don't belong here. How about you move on?'

'I guess we got us a standoff then,' Tyler said. He gave an almost imperceptible nod and there was movement behind Curtis.

El Tigre had noticed it and his head snapped around. He brought the Yellow Boy back and up at an angle so that the butt plate caught Bower flush in the face before the man could crack him with the handle in his grasp.

Bower's jaw gave way under the brutal blow and blood gushed from his ruined mouth. The big man collapsed to his knees, dropping his weapon.

Sweeping the Winchester forward again, Curtis looped his finger through the trigger and fired it. The slug caught Tyler in the throat and tore through it with little resistance. Bright crimson sprayed from a torn artery on to the ground as the foreman tried to stem the flow with one hand in a losing battle.

He dropped the axe he was holding, his second hand failing to do what the first one couldn't. He was dead in no time.

Curtis jacked another round into the breech of the Yellow Boy and shot another lumberjack trying to brain him with a branch. The bullet slammed into the man's middle where it deflected downward off his bottom rib. The twisted hunk of metal ripped through soft flesh and tissue, creating a wound from which the man would never recover.

A fourth man moved in with an axe and was stopped mid-swing when the hot barrel of the Winchester pressed hard against his forehead. A bead of sweat formed on his brow as soon as he realized he was in trouble. El Tigre's voice was cold, menacing. 'I wouldn't.'

The Yellow Boy was in his right hand and with his left, Curtis drew the Remington. He pointed it at another lumberjack just in case more of them had any ideas.

'What's it going to be?' he asked.

The man with the Yellow Boy pressed to his forehead swallowed hard and said, 'I'm done.'

'Uh huh,' Curtis said then ran his gaze over the others. 'What about the rest of you? You done too?'

There were murmurs of agreement from them.

'OK. This is what you're going to do. I want all of your axes and other equipment put in a pile over there,' he pointed with the Remington to a small cleared area not far from the mill.

Once they'd finished, Curtis said, 'Burn it.'

Two of them set the small pile on fire and stood back.

Curtis nodded. 'Now the machinery.'

This time they hesitated. One of them said, 'Are you crazy? We can't burn that. Brotherton has a lot of money tied up in that.'

'His problem, not mine. Burn it.'

The man shook his head. 'Nope. You want it done, do it yourself.'

El Tigre shot him with the Remington. Not dead, just in the leg as an example for the others.

He lay squirming on the ground, clutching at the wound in his thigh. His face was bright red and he managed, 'Damn you, you son-of-a-bitch!'

Curtis ignored him and stared down the remainder of the men. 'Anyone else have an issue?'

143

'I'll do it,' a solid man growled. 'Didn't much like working for the son-of-a-bitch anyway.'

'I'll help you,' said another man.

There was a moan from Bower. Curtis glanced at him but saw him go still again as the darkness of unconsciousness claimed him.

Before long the machinery was aflame, and a pall of smoke billowed into the blue sky. The men who'd started the fire stepped back.

'All right,' Curtis said. 'All of you get moving back to town. Tell Brotherton it finishes today. And take your trash with you.'

CHAPTER 16

The rider entered the Circle M yard and eased his horse to a stop. He waited a few moments before climbing down. As he did, the sun reflected off the badge pinned to his shirt.

The door opened on the ranch house and Beth Morris and Mary-Alice appeared. They eyed him with caution and Beth asked, 'What do you want, Sheriff Reynolds?'

'I came to see if Curtis was here,' he answered.

'Well, he ain't,' Mary-Alice said.

'I see that. When are you expecting him back?'

'What makes you think he's coming back?'

'You do. You're here. He's made himself your protector. Both of you really. That's how I know he'll be back.'

'You're wrong,' Beth told him.

'We'll see, shall we?' Reynolds said, leading his horse towards the water trough. He paused for a moment as hands began to gather. 'Are your men going to be a problem?'

'Not unless I tell them to be,' Beth answered.

'Fine. I'll wait over here.'

Mary-Alice stepped forward. 'Why are you doing this? You're supposed to be his friend.'

'I was once. Things change.'

'So now you're here to kill him?'

'It's what I'm being paid to do.'

'What if he kills you?'

'Then I'll be dead. Anything else?'

Mary-Alice shook her head. 'No.'

When Curtis approached the Circle M yard he could see that all the hands were gathered outside. Immediately he knew that something wasn't right. He took the Yellow Boy from its scabbard and cocked the hammer. With that done he laid it across his thighs, his right hand continuing to grip it while his left controlled the reins.

The roan walked into the yard and he drew it to a halt. No sooner had the animal stopped when Mary-Alice ran up to him, panic in her eyes.

'You have to leave,' she blurted out. 'Go now, he's here to kill you.'

Curtis knew who she meant but still he asked her, 'Who is?'

She turned her head and at last, he saw the figure over at the water trough. Reynolds started walking towards him. Curtis gripped the Winchester and a hint of regret ran through him at what was about to happen.

'I sure wish you hadn't come, Captain,' Curtis said.

146

'And I wish it could be another way, Jim, but it can't be. It's come too far.'

'I guess it has,' Curtis acknowledged. 'Give me a minute to get down?'

Reynolds shrugged. 'Sure.'

He climbed from the roan and gave the animal a push on its rump. It moved away, leaving the two men facing each other. Curtis moved to his left a fraction to get the sun out of his eyes.

'How do you want to do this, Captain?'

'What about we get the lady to call it? Make it even.'

Curtis stared at Reynolds awhile before nodding. 'All right. We'll do it that way.'

'No, I won't,' Mary-Alice said.

'Just do it,' Curtis snapped. 'Either way, this finishes here.'

She hesitated, not wanting to be the reason for men dying. 'All right. I'll do it.'

The tension grew while both men waited for her to give the word. The silence was palpable and the only thing that could be heard was the buzz of a fly.

Still Mary-Alice remained silent.

Then, without waiting, Curtis moved. The Yellow Boy came up into its firing position and bucked in his hands. The move caught Reynolds off guard and the slug smashed into his chest, burned deep, and exploded out of his back.

Reynolds' jaw dropped with disbelief at the way Curtis had played it. His eyes bulged and he staggered slightly.

'Sorry, Captain,' Curtis said. 'But like you said, war

147

changes a man.'

With slow deliberate movements, he worked the lever, and the Yellow Boy was ready to fire once more.

Reynolds fought to get his six-gun out of its holster, but fumbled with it, then gave up. He lurched to the side and stared at his former sergeant. He gave him half a smile and closed his eyes.

The Yellow Boy whiplashed, and Reynolds fell, dead before he hit the ground.

The sound of the last shot rolled across the landscape until fading away amongst the distant hills, lost amongst the tall pines. It was followed by a drawn-out silence while the watchers struggled to comprehend the violence they'd just witnessed.

It was Beth who spoke first. 'You didn't give him a chance. He was your friend and you didn't give him a chance.'

Curtis stared at her and said, 'He would have done the same to me, given the chance. As for being my friend, that was a long time ago.'

'But it was so cold.'

'That's killing. There's nothing warm about it.'

'What do we do now?' Mary-Alice asked.

'Sling him over his horse. I'll take him to town with me.'

'You're going to town?'

'Uh huh. This needs to end. Brotherton is the only outstanding problem that's left. Now that his two main hired guns are dead, he's vulnerable.'

Curtis walked away from them and headed towards the stables.

148

'Where are you going?'

'Get a horse.'

Mary-Alice watched in silence as he packed things into his saddle-bags, then placed his bedroll behind his saddle. With that done, Curtis rechecked his saddle and stuffed his Yellow Boy into the saddle scabbard.

'You aren't coming back, are you?' It was more a statement than a question.

He turned and looked her in the eyes, noticing that they were starting to fill with tears. Curtis nodded. 'That's right.'

'But why?'

'It's time for me to move on. Once this is done, you'll be fine. You can rebuild, make a life for you and Lester.'

'How can I rebuild if I have no money?'

'You have all of that timber on your land. You know what it's worth. Sell some of it and you'll have all you need.'

She moved in close to him and grasped his arms. 'What if I ask you to stay with me?'

A soft smile appeared on Curtis' face. He gently pushed her away from him. 'I'm sorry, Mary-Alice. As good as that sounds, it can never be. You deserve better than me.'

Anger flared in her eyes. 'Like Lester?'

'Yes. He's a good man. He cares for you, Mary-Alice. You could do a lot worse.'

'I want to do worse. I want you, damn it.'

'I can't.'

'Why not, damn you?'

'It's a long story.'

'I'm listening.'

Curtis hesitated. He looked into her eyes and found himself saying. 'I had a woman. Down in Mexico. She was the most beautiful person I'd ever known. Her name was Nita. We had a son, too. His name was Emilio. We had a small house, not much really, but it was home. Someone found out who I was. The famous El Tigre. Whoever it was told the soldiers about me. We were asleep the night they came for me. But they weren't happy with killing me, they wanted more. They killed Nita and Emilio. It was only by chance that I didn't die too. I might as well have.'

Mary-Alice reached out and placed a gentle hand on his arm. 'How terrible it must have been. I'm sorry.'

Curtis shrugged it off. 'That's why I can't stay. Like I said, Lester is a good man, he'll make you a good husband.'

Realizing that what he said was true, she moved in close and wrapped her arms around him. Her closeness almost made him uncomfortable. Mary-Alice raised herself up and kissed him on his stubbled cheek. She stepped back and said, 'Thank you. For everything. If it wasn't for you I'd probably still be in Opal.'

He grabbed up the reins of Reynolds' horse and climbed into his own saddle. Once he was comfortable he reached down and touched Mary-Alice on the cheek. 'Say goodbye to Beth for me.'

She nodded. 'Be careful, Jim.'

He straightened up and swung the roan away. As he rode out of the yard, she stared long and hard at his back, wishing that he would turn around and come back.

Behind Mary-Alice the door on the house opened. She turned to see Beth standing on the veranda, then make her way down the steps and cross to where Mary-Alice stood. They wrapped their arms around each other as Beth said, 'He didn't say goodbye.'

Without taking her eyes off Curtis, Mary-Alice said, 'You knew?'

'Had a feeling.'

'I hope he lives through this to keep going.'

'I have a feeling he will. Men like Jim Curtis are hard to kill.'

CHAPTER 17

Curtis stopped the roan at the edge of town and released Reynolds' horse. He slapped it on the rump and it trotted into town, much to the shock of many of the townsfolk, who stopped to stare at the horse with the body draped over it.

Curtis, however, used the distraction to slip into town on foot, unnoticed. He figured that Brotherton would be at the Silver Aspen, so he moved along the back street until he was at the back of the hotel. He tried the rear door but found it locked. 'Guess I won't be going that way again,' he murmured.

Moving along to the side alley, Curtis found a set of stairs that led up to the second floor of the saloon. He climbed to the top of them and tried the door. It snicked open and he stepped through the opening.

The hallway was narrow and dim, the walls lined with wallpaper and dark timber panelling. With slow, deliberate steps he made his way along the hall. When he reached halfway, a door to his left opened and a scantily-clad whore with dark hair, wearing only under-wear and a corset, emerged.

She saw the Yellow Boy in his hands and opened her mouth to scream. Curtis clasped a hand over her gaping mouth and cut it off. He whispered, 'Don't. I'm only here for Brotherton. Is he downstairs?'

With eyes wide, she shook her head.

'He's not?'

She shrugged.

He took his hand away and she spoke with a trembling voice, 'I don't know.'

Curtis flicked his eyes towards the room she'd appeared from and said, 'Go back inside the room. At least for a while, anyway.'

She understood what he was saying and retreated the way she'd come. The door closed behind her and Curtis kept walking.

On reaching the landing, he paused. The whole bar room was visible from where he stood, and he took time to run his gaze over it, unobserved.

And there was Brotherton, sitting at a table with three other men. Big men. Most likely men from his mill. The room was half full, being late in the afternoon. Cigarette smoke was starting to fill it like an early morning mist, and as the night wore on it would only get worse.

The saloon doors crashed open as Curtis was about to cross to the head of the stairs. A man stopped just inside and shouted above the din, 'The sheriff's been shot! He's dead!'

There was uproar in the saloon and chairs scraped

back as men, those who were seated, climbed hurriedly to their feet. Brotherton was amongst them.

Curtis watched them jam out through the door and he started down the steps. Once at the bottom he began to cross the room, weaving his way between tables and chairs. He paused before exiting the saloon. Staring out at the crowd on the street, he could hear raised voices as men checked out Reynolds' corpse.

'I want that bastard found!' Brotherton's curse was audible above the rest of the voices. 'I'll pay one thousand dollars to any man who brings me his damn head.'

Voices grew louder as others started to incite more from the crowd. The group began to disperse, leaving Brotherton and his three men standing on the street. Curtis heard him say, 'Now we'll get the son-of-a-bitch.'

Curtis cocked the hammer on the Yellow Boy and stepped out on to the boardwalk. 'I won't be too hard to locate.'

Brotherton's eyes widened when he realized who it was. 'You!'

One of the men beside the timber man panicked and grasped for the butt of his gun. The Winchester moved, and Curtis shot him in the chest. He didn't worry nor care about shooting him again. The man was hit hard enough to stay down.

Curtis shifted aim as he jacked another round into the Winchester's breech. The hammer fell on the .44 Henry cartridge and a second man fell. Baring his teeth, El Tigre repeated it once more. When he'd finished, the three men with Brotherton were down in the dirt. Two writhed in pain, while the third was unmoving.

Another bullet was rammed home and the foresight of the Yellow Boy settled on the pale face of Brotherton.

The dispersal of the crowd had stalled with the sound of gunfire, and people were now beginning to regather.

'There's the bastard,' someone called out. 'He killed our sheriff and now he's killed three more men. Shoot him, quick.'

'Wait!' Brotherton shrieked. 'Don't you see where he's got that gun pointed?'

'He's right,' another man shouted. 'He's got it pointed at Mr Brotherton.'

The crowd closed in and Curtis snapped, 'That's far enough. I ain't afraid to kill more of you. Including Brotherton.'

'Stop!' Brotherton blurted out. 'He'll do it. He's a killer.'

They did as they were told. Curtis ran his gaze over the faces. He said, 'I want you all to hear something. When Doug Morris died, he left his ranch to his daughter, Beth. Cody was left with nothing. Which meant that he couldn't sell the timber on the Circle M range to Brotherton.'

'How do you know?' a man asked. 'The will was never found.'

Curtis noticed the slight smile that touched

Brotherton's lips.

'Beth has the will at her place.'

'It has to be fake,' Brotherton sneered. 'Why would she have it and not come forward?'

'I found it,' Curtis said.

'Where?' a voice asked.

'Yes, where?' Brotherton demanded.

Flint-hard eyes settled on the timber man. 'In Brotherton's office, right before I burned it.'

A murmur rippled through the crowd.

'Lies!' Brotherton snapped. 'All lies.'

Ignoring him, Curtis continued. 'Cody killed his own father. Why? I can only assume that he and Brotherton had some kind of deal worked out, because no sooner was Doug Morris dead, Cody sold the timber rights to Brotherton.'

'Don't believe him,' Brotherton pleaded.

'Every bad thing that has happened lately is because of Brotherton. The sheriff being killed so he could bring in his own man to replace him, Hennessy the livery owner was killed by Vince. Mary-Alice's spread was burned and most of the cattle shot, even the stage hold-up was done on his say-so. But the killing didn't start here. It began months ago in a town called Opal, near Abilene. That was where Andrews shot and killed Mary-Alice's husband because they were coming here to take up land. Land that Brotherton wanted for its timber.'

'Lies!' Brotherton shrieked, spittle flying from his lips. 'Lies! Can't you see? He's the killer. Not me. I've killed no one.'

156

'The only liar here is you,' Curtis said to him. 'But now, it's all over. You're finished.'

'The only one around here that's finished, you bastard, is you,' Brotherton cried out and his hand went for his gun.

The man was so worked up that he fumbled it before he got it halfway clear of leather. Then, once it did clear, he dropped it because his hands were shaking so much. He looked up and saw the Yellow Boy still trained on his chest. He glanced up at Curtis and gave him a half smile.

El Tigre bared his teeth, and Brotherton died.

The Yellow Boy roared for one final time and the slug burned deep into the timber man's chest. He collapsed on to the street and didn't move.

Curses from the crowd brought the Winchester around to cover a group of four men who tried to surge forward. 'I wouldn't if I were you.'

'Do you think you'll get out of town alive?'

'He will,' another voice grated.

The group turned to face the new challenge. This one carried a cut-down messenger gun. Which made him formidable even though he was in a wheelchair. Lester said, 'Any one of you so much as moves, I'll unload both barrels.'

Curtis smiled to himself. Lester had come a long way.

'You all right, Jim?' he asked.

'Yeah, fine.'

'All right you hombres, get the hell off the street. This man just saved your damned town from a wolf in

157

sheep's clothing.'

They frowned at him and he snapped, 'Get! Go on.'

The crowd dispersed.

'Hold it! You timber men are forgetting something. Clean your leavings off the street.'

Curtis watched on as the bodies of the dead were cleared away, and then he walked over to where Lester and the doctor were. 'Thanks for that. I guess I owe you.'

'Owe me, be damned. You've taught me a lot in a short piece of time.'

Holding out his right hand, Curtis said, 'I'll be seeing you, Lester.'

Lester frowned. 'Are you leaving?'

'Yeah. Time to move on. It's all over. Brotherton is dead, so are his gun hands.'

'What about Mary-Alice?'

'What about her?'

'Does she know you're leaving?'

'She does. I've said my goodbyes. You take good care of her.'

Lester nodded. 'Take care, Jim. Don't forget to come back and visit.'

'I'll do that,' Curtis said, but he knew, as did Lester, that it wouldn't happen. ' 'Bye, Doc.'

' 'Bye, Jim.'

Lester watched him walk away along the main street. He turned his head back to the doctor and said, 'Can we go back now?'

'Sure.'

*

When Curtis reached the outskirts of town where he'd left the roan, he slid the Yellow Boy back into the saddle scabbard and climbed into the saddle. He sat there for a moment looking back along the street. He could just make out the doctor wheeling Lester away.

'I guess we're done, horse,' he said. 'Come on, let's ride.'

Turning the roan about, he pointed him east. Maybe this time he'd reach Abilene.